Vision Captured

LORIE O'CLARE

ELLORA'S CAVE
ROMANTICA PUBLISHING

What the critics are saying...

❦

"*Vision Captured* is another stellar book by Lorie O' Clare. In keeping with her other shifter series' this book is the first in what is sure to be another group of great stories. Lori gives you just enough to wrap up the story line, but also leaves enough unanswered questions to be sure that you will just have to buy the next one to see what happens. I can't wait."

~ *Manic Readers*

An Ellora's Cave Romantica Publication

www.ellorascave.com

Vision Captured

ISBN 9781419959332
ALL RIGHTS RESERVED.
Vision Captured Copyright © 2008 Lorie O'Clare
Edited by Mary Moran.
Cover art by Syneca.

This book printed in the U.S.A. by Jasmine-Jade Enterprises, LLC.

Electronic book Publication August 2008
Trade paperback Publication June 2009

VISION CAPTURED

&

Chapter One

ಐ

"He doesn't exist." Chantelle Drap focused on the sound her boots made on the sidewalk. "It's just bullshit to scare us. Make us submit."

Chan didn't submit to anyone. She didn't care about rumors claiming some ghost wanted to control leopards. There was no Leo Pard. It was impossible to unify leopards, say who would live where, or with whom. They weren't fucking werewolves, or like some of the other species who lived together in packs. Hell, Chan didn't even know any other leopards in Seattle. Which was fine with her. And it's how it would stay. No one controlled leopards. And no one would ever control her!

At the intersection, she watched headlights create glossy blurs of brightness over the soaked street from the heavy downpour. Water gurgled as it ran into the gutters. At the first break in traffic, she ignored the red light and hurried across the street. Raindrops clung to her eyelashes and streamed down her cheeks. She didn't duck, but kept up her pace, her head held high as she watched the shadows.

Her apartment complex wasn't too far from the factory, and when she worked the late shift, jogging home helped clear her head. Tonight, enjoying the rain, and all the fresh scents it brought on, put her in a good mood. She didn't mind the smell of humans everywhere. They were harmless half creatures who were too wrapped up in their own lives to notice she wasn't one of them.

"Although maybe that's how it is with all of us," she mused as she noted how slick the cement stairs to her complex building were from the rain. It wasn't as if she paid much attention to the problems humans claimed to have.

Ignoring the rows of mailboxes in the wall just inside the small foyer, she headed for the stairs. If there were any truth to the ridiculous slander she read on the Panthera Incognita website, she would find out soon. Most of the time the website didn't impress her. A password-protected site, PI was a place where leopards could announce any bit of news they wished other leopards to know. The site was full of ads, property for sale, or job listings. Once in a while single males, or females, would announce their desire to find a mate, or a partner for some "no strings attached" fun. The ads reeked of lies even through the Internet.

"If some of those ads were true," she growled under her breath, she'd jump on the opportunity to enjoy a good romp with some gorgeous rogue male. None of the ads were ever in Seattle though. The sexy rogue usually turned out to be washed up and barely functional anymore. Not that she would respond to some blind request on PI for a leopard to get a piece of tail, but it was what she'd heard.

The mating ads weren't what bothered her tonight though. She didn't have much time on her lunch break to read over the website carefully. No one complained about the employees using the computers in the office during breaks. But she didn't want some busybody human asking what she was doing, or getting curious about which websites she cruised.

"Give anyone reason to gossip," she grumbled, knowing all too well that humans jumped on the chance to create scandal about each other. No way would she get caught in their crossfire if one of them saw her at a website that discussed people who were also leopards.

Which was why she needed to get on her laptop, so she could better read the announcement she barely managed to glance at while at work. In spite of her determination to believe the announcement was pure bullshit, this was the first time Chan ever heard of other leopards claiming to see visions—to see the future before it happened. Up until now, she thought she was the only one.

Chan didn't bother holding on to the banister as she marched up the two flights to her floor. Her heart raced but it wasn't from flying up the stairs. Maybe she read the announcement wrong. After all, rumors of a male named Leo Pard smelled stale these days. There had been talk of him when she was a cub.

"I probably read it wrong." After all, she opened the website, glanced at the main page and clicked out of it before anyone saw her there. "He's a joke, a ghost," she reminded herself. "None of this can be true anyway. Even if there were others out there like me, I sure as hell wouldn't let someone take me away from my home because I see things." No one knew Chan saw the future. No one. Not even her own litter. "So there's nothing to worry about."

Not that she cared about anything on PI. Granted, she was damn glad humans couldn't smell emotions when she first glimpsed at the main page of the website. Every one of them would have been breathing down her neck, dying to know what stunned the fucking hell out of her. And they said curiosity killed cats.

Chan reached the top of the stairs and pulled the second-floor door open. All she would do was reread the headline that mentioned gathering all leopards who saw visions into one place, make sure she read it right, and then she would leave that damn site alone. Curiosity wouldn't get her ass killed. She wasn't getting gathered up, or taken off anywhere.

The heavy door opened toward her and Chan saw down the long, narrow hallway with apartment doors on either side. She almost staggered when she breathed in the raw, musky scent of a male leopard.

She didn't smell a female on him. Hissing, but then gulping in more of his feral, untamed aroma, she stared at the single male rogue who stood halfway down the hallway.

What the fuck? God damn he smelled good. He was tall and well built. Her own scent changed instantly as desire swelled inside her. She'd gone way too long without indulging in some good, rough sex.

Chan recovered quickly and walked with determination to her apartment. As if any male—drop-dead gorgeous or not—would ever see her hesitate. Chan didn't know of any single male leopards in Seattle, but she hadn't invited him here and therefore he didn't merit her attention.

"Chantelle Drap?" he asked, his smooth baritone sending chills over her flesh and creating a burning sensation inside her that spread like wildfire throughout her insides.

"Nope." She shoved her key into lock, turned it, pushed open her door and then entered the safety of her dark apartment. Looking over her shoulder and glaring at him, she gripped her door handle, adrenaline pumping harder and faster until she could hardly breathe.

The male turned, thumbs hooked in his jeans, and stared at her with wild green eyes. Sparks shot up her spine as the urge to attack, taste him, demand that he mount her, made it almost impossible to move.

But she did. She clicked the lock into place, shrugged out of her coat and then bent over to pull off her boots, all the while fighting the trembling need that made her excited and anxious. Small puddles of water pooled at her feet. She turned, listening to the silence.

The male still stood outside her door. She smelled him but didn't hear him. Which disturbed her. What the fuck did he want?

"Why does shit always hit all at once?" she whispered, and then cocked her head, listening.

Nothing.

"Stand out there all night. See if I care." She knew he heard her, yet he didn't pound her door down. Nor did he leave.

Single males were nomadic, rogues. Most of them took what they wanted, and none of them could be trusted. Her breed might be condemned for that fact, but that didn't make it less true. Until a female was intrigued enough by a male to attempt conquering him, forcing his submission to her, he was dangerous and to be avoided at all costs. The way Chan saw it, no male was worth conquering. Some good sparring and hot sex once in a while worked fine with her, but then they could just go sniff somewhere else and leave her alone.

She headed to her kitchen, flipped the light on and stared at her reflection in her large window. A steak and beer, her laptop, and hopefully some answers were in strong order. She opened the refrigerator, pulled out a plate with a couple slabs of meat on it and popped it into the microwave. Grabbing her beer, Chan sat down at the kitchen table and opened her laptop while nervous anticipation attacked with such a vengeance that she shook. This male outside her door didn't simply show up on the off chance of getting his dick wet.

She remembered the headline she saw briefly on the main page of PI. *Leopards With Visions Being Gathered...*

"Like fucking hell," she growled, and almost bit the tip of her beer bottle. No one knew she saw things other leopards didn't. No one. "That isn't why he's here."

Chan heard the double click a second before the microwave beeped. Her doorknob turned, making a protesting sound as the lock snapped, broke, and the door opened with a quiet squeak. Heavy footsteps moved slowly into her living room.

Instantly his powerful scent, one that was aggressive, dominating and definitely all male, filled her apartment and sent her heart beating at a pace almost too fast for her human body to handle. Tingles prickled over her flesh and her insides swelled as sexual need attacked her harder than she ever remembered feeling it before. She slammed her fist against the table, dwelling on the pain and the fact she'd just been violated by unwelcome company. No rogue male would break into her home and then make her weak in the knees.

She stood, gathering inner strength, and walked with slow determination out of the kitchen. "You are going to pay to fix that lock," she snarled.

"You won't need the lock." He didn't hide his thumbs in his jeans pockets any longer, but stopped in the middle of the living room, hands on hips, glancing around at the pictures on her walls, her furniture and finally at her. Bright green flickered with streaks of gold as he devoured her with the gaze of a victorious predator. His intense stare seemed to stop time, and a twisting pressure in her gut made it hard to breathe.

"Let's go," he growled, barely moving his mouth.

Chan forced a laugh, reminding herself that no matter his overwhelming sex appeal, he'd broken into her home and needed to be taught manners. "Like hell. Get the hell out of my apartment before I kick you out."

"I can't leave you here alone, Chantelle. You're coming with me."

Her microwave beeped again and she turned her back on him, letting him know with her body language that he wouldn't intimidate her. Her heart pounded hard enough to create a rushing sound in her head though. Who the fuck was he? "Leo Pard hired me to find you," the male said, his musky aroma growing stronger as he followed her into the kitchen.

If he saw her reaction to that name, it would have been two points for him. And she shook out of rage, not fear. There wasn't any reason to fear a leopard who didn't exist.

Chan didn't drop the plate as she pulled it out of the microwave. Setting it next to her laptop, she barely smelled the steak over his all-male scent. She focused on the moisture from the beer bottle tickling her fingers as drops created paths to her palm while bringing it to her lips. His gaze grew hooded as his lashes sloped over his intense green eyes and he watched her drink.

"I'm not sure I think much of a male who takes orders from a ghost," she said, licking her lips and gaining a warped sense of power when he focused on her tongue gliding over her lips.

He was even sexier when he smiled. His eyes flashed with amusement and his curly hair, damp from the rain, was a mixture of blond and red. He was muscular, but most single males his age were. A rogue, nomadic, who would appear, do damage or good, and then disappear once they broke a female's heart, unless she decided to tame him.

"I don't take orders."

"Of course you don't." She sat at her table, forcing her attention on her laptop, steak and beer. "You aren't welcome in my home. Leave."

She stared at the PI main page, once again seeing the bold headline— *Leopards With Visions Will Be Gathered.*

The beer she swallowed churned cruelly in her gut. The paragraph she didn't have time to read at work stated simply— *For the better of all leopards, Leo Pard announces the protection and training of selected males and females who are gifted with seeing into the future. Names have been selected. Hunters are gathering these females and males. They will be collared and trained. From this day forward, leopards will be the strongest panthera, a species who will be honored and feared worldwide.*

"Does that scare you?" he asked quietly, his tone a mixture between a whisper and a growl. "I didn't come here to get kicked out," he informed her. She caught him in her peripheral vision, leaning in her doorway and crossing his muscular arms over his chest. "You need protection," he informed her.

"Nothing scares me and I'm not convinced I even need protection from you," she snarled.

The male leapt across her kitchen. "Then let me convince you," he hissed, his tone turning dark and menacing.

15

Chan leapt out of her chair when he attacked. In spite of the height difference, she didn't hesitate. Growling fiercely, anticipating his actions, adrenaline kicked in full force with a harsh punch.

"All you're convincing me of is that I need to throw you out instead of asking you to go away," she howled, and dodged when he tried to grab her.

"I'm not leaving." He turned quickly, his blond-red hair falling partially over his face as he dove to the side.

She tried racing out of the kitchen, but he grabbed her. With a good six inches in height on her and possibly a hundred pounds heavier, Chan wouldn't stand a chance if he pinned her. She twisted furiously and managed to hit him in the side of the head with her elbow.

He simply growled louder. "He told me you'd be a feisty, stubborn bitch," the male snarled, his large hands snaking around her waist.

Chan wondered who in the hell "he" was. But if she exerted energy on conversation, she would lose the fight. And she seriously doubted this male took orders from, or had ever spoken to, Leo Pard. There was no such male. If there were, someone would have found him by now for all of his claims to unite a species that simply couldn't be united.

"You should have listened," she snapped, and managed to squirm out of his hands.

Without hesitating, she jumped into the air and used the strongest part of her body, her legs. She kicked hard, made contact. Bone hit bone with a nasty crunching sound. Chan fell backward, hitting her kitchen wall and damn near knocking herself unconscious. She slid down to her butt and took a moment to let her vision clear. Then wiping hair from her face, she reached up for her beer and took a long swallow.

The male hunched over, his hand covering his jaw where she'd kicked. When he straightened, raising his gaze to hers, the fiery glow in his eyes stole her breath. It had been way too long since she'd seriously kicked someone's ass. And she wouldn't even dwell on how long it was since she'd last been laid. But mix a bit of violence with some hot, rough sex, and a leopard's paradise was found.

Dangerous territory. Very dangerous territory. She pushed herself to her feet, still holding her beer while watching him warily.

"You're the one who's going to listen," he sneered. His roguish features turned menacing.

The male jumped but she darted around him, barely making time to put down her beer before flying into her living room. She didn't get far. He pounced on her back, his arms wrapping around her and constricting the air out of her lungs. They tumbled to the floor, and with his weight on top of her, she fell hard.

"God damn it!" she yelled, turning her head, and then reluctantly rested her cheek against her carpet.

"Are you convinced now?" He adjusted his body so his legs trapped hers and the rest of him pressed against her backside.

"Convinced that you're fucking insane," she snarled, unable to even lift herself off the floor. He outweighed her twice over.

"Any male would fight for you, Chantelle."

"You aren't fighting for me, you're fighting against me." She hated how he used her formal name, letting it glide off his tongue with a smoothness that annoyed her. "And quit calling me that."

"It's your name." He pushed his body off her with one arm but kept his legs on top of hers. "Why would I call you anything else?"

"Only my litter calls me that. You don't have the right." There wasn't a worse feeling on the planet than that of being trapped. She squirmed underneath him, wishing for the muscle to send him flying.

17

Something hard and long suddenly pressed against her ass, thick, warm and very, very dangerous-feeling.

Chan quit moving.

He chuckled, a deep, blood-chilling sound that at the same time created a rush of heat inside her. She lifted her head, straining to look over her shoulder.

No fucking way in hell would he sense any emotion he could use against her. "Get the fuck off me," she demanded.

Surprisingly, he obliged, rising to his feet and lifting her to hers. She tried moving away from him, but he grabbed her arms, turning her around. Her hair fell over part of her face and she couldn't free her arms to move the mass out of the way.

So she glared at him through it.

"I guess it makes sense he wouldn't tell me how fucking hot you are," he said quietly.

"Who is he?"

"Charles."

Chan blinked. The only Charles she knew was her littermate in Phoenix. It had been almost three years since she talked to Charles. He probably didn't even know how to reach her.

"So Leo Pard's real name is Charles?" she asked, playing stupid and praying he would say something that would make sense. Although if he simply came here to fuck her, he would say anything just to confuse her more and distract her so she couldn't fight.

His gaze dropped down her body while his fingers moved slightly on her arms, scalding her flesh and causing tingles to rush just underneath her flesh. "Leo's name is Leo, and Charles' name is Charles," he said as if that explained everything. There was no smell of amusement on him in spite of his calm, soothing tone. If anything, his scent turned muskier the longer he stood holding her arms.

18

She wasn't going to stand here and wait for him to make sense. Her right arm burned when she yanked it free of his grip, but he managed to pull her into his arms before she could create any space between them. When she almost tripped over her coffee table, he picked her up, slamming her backside against his rock-hard chest.

"Let me go," she spat while fierce sparks sliced through her spine. The change begged to be released inside her. As a leopard she was stronger, faster, and could kill so much easier.

"I will when you calm down," he whispered into her hair. "The way you're squirming, you're making me think you like rubbing your ass up against my cock."

"Why you…" Outrage exploded inside her and she twisted furiously, kicking with her legs and digging her nails into his arms. She wouldn't be humiliated. And if he planned on mounting her, he wouldn't survive it unscathed.

"Chantelle, you can't overpower me." His breath scorched her neck.

And she hated being told she couldn't do something. She bent her knees, moving fast and using every bit of strength she could muster without changing from her human form. His hands slid over her, brushing her breasts. Her nipples turned so hard they ached. She ignored the change in the aroma surrounding them. Even though hostile emotions hung heavy with their pungent smells, there was something else rich and sweet—the smell of lust.

If she didn't put space between them immediately, he would fuck her. Every instinct inside her screamed to take him on, demand he fuck her, gain the upper paw. Then he would have to submit to her. But her human side insisted she maintain control of the situation and keep her clothes on.

Chan moved quickly. She squatted and pulled his body over with all her might. Yanking on his shoulders, she roared as she took on his weight, knocked him off balance and then threw him over her.

Chan flipped him over her shoulder and then scurried backward as quickly as she could without falling over. Every inch of her sizzled with raw, unleashed energy. His massive frame shook her home with the impact. She almost tripped over her own feet when she tightened every muscle and forced herself not to leap on him. Chan wanted the fight, the physical contact. It was in her nature, and it was damned hard to curb the burning excitement inside her.

She slapped her hand against the wall next to her kitchen door to stabilize herself and watched as he picked himself up off the floor.

"Little bitch," he snarled.

"You asked for it." She would throw him out of her apartment, but since he'd broken the lock, it would be a futile effort. "Why are you here?"

"I told you. I was sent..."

"I know. Don't feed me your Leo Pard crap. He's a ghost, an urban legend who doesn't exist. And don't make up other names just to appease me. If you're going to force yourself into my home and then put your paws all over me, at least honor me with the truth."

He reclined on her couch and combed his hair with his fingers. When he looked up at her, he slowly rubbed his jaw where she'd kicked him, and then twisted and popped his back.

"My paws wouldn't have been on you if you didn't attack me."

"I wouldn't have attacked if you'd behaved like an honorable leopard," she spat.

His hair was still tousled when he looked up at her and grinned slowly. "If I didn't have honor, I would have taken you out in the hallway without bothering to come in and explain the situation before we leave."

"I've already made it damn clear I'm not going anywhere." She fought not to stare, or worse yet, start drooling when he reclined comfortably on her couch. Roped muscles pressed against denim. His cock was still hard and pressed against his jeans. Definitely not a sight she could focus on and keep her wits about her. Chan paced the length of her living room to her front door. "I'll allow you to display this honor you claim to have. Tell me why you're here. What do you want? And don't leave out any details."

"Leo Pard hired all of the hunters to come get you as well as others. You read the message on Panthera Incognita. Charles, your littermate in Phoenix, is a good and honorable male. He's mated to my littermate Jenny. When I took the job, I learned your name was on the list. Charles and I agreed you must be protected until we know more about what Leo plans on doing with the males and females he's gathering. Call your littermate if you must." He stopped talking and watched her with a hooded gaze that simply added to his incredible good looks.

"Go on," she said, focusing on her breathing and refusing to let him smell nervousness on her, or worse yet, lust.

He stood slowly, watching her with those damnable green eyes that darkened as he lazily moved closer. She wouldn't give him any indication of her next move, but she could dive for her door and be out of there in seconds if needed. Although where the hell would she run?

"You're not safe here any longer," he said quietly. "I think I've just proven that. If I wanted, I could have fucked you and you wouldn't have been able to stop me. So I'm here to get you and take you with me. Another hunter might not be as concerned about your reputation."

She raised one eyebrow. "You're mighty sure of yourself, male. I just kicked your ass, not the other way around."

Even though she was ready for him to leap, she couldn't dive for the door fast enough. He grabbed her, lifted her off the ground and threw her onto the couch. In the next instant, he landed on top of her, pinning her hands above her head. Her breasts smashed against rock-hard muscle. His cock was engorged and throbbed between them. He pinned her legs, rendering her trapped. His face was inches from hers, and he lowered it so his lips brushed over hers. She turned her head, refusing to simply submit just because he demanded it.

His breath scorched her skin, raising the tiny hairs on her flesh when his lips moved over her ear. "I didn't kick your ass because I wouldn't hurt you. And if I wanted you without your consent, I would already be inside you."

Chapter Two

❧

Charles Drap had done a piss-poor job of describing his littermate to Josh Bard. Josh distinctly remembered Charles saying his littermate was reclusive and serious by nature. He blamed it on some trauma she'd experienced as a cub. Now that Josh thought about it, maybe he'd concluded from Charles' description that Chantelle would be plain-looking, unappealing. The fiery little cat underneath him was just about the hottest fucking female he'd ever sniffed out.

"I've never taken anything that wasn't offered. And if you keep fighting me like this, I'll know there's more on your mind than chasing my tail out of here." He loved a female who knew how to wear makeup, and Chantelle's pale brown eye shadow made her green eyes larger, more seductive.

"You're hurting me," she grumbled, and turned her head to look at the living room, making a show of not giving him her attention in spite of the fact their legs were intertwined.

"I doubt that very much." Her nipples were hard pebbles against his chest and distracted the hell out of him. But her soft body, curvy and slender, draped underneath him, made it damned impossible to think. He kept his weight off her, flexing his arms so their flesh brushed over each other, and she could easily move underneath him, torture the fucking hell out of him, but not escape.

She turned her head just enough to glare at him. "Get the fuck off me," she growled.

He thought about ignoring her command, pushing her just a bit to see when she would break. He wasn't lying to her. She needed protection, serious protection, and soon. In order to ensure her safety, he needed her trust. Seducing her into

23

trusting him sounded damn appealing. But in spite of her inaccurate conclusions of him, he was a leopard with honor.

Josh moved to his knees and took her hand to pull her into a sitting position next to him. Her legs remained trapped on either side of him though.

"Feel better?" he asked.

"Hell no. Who the hell are you?"

"Joshua Bard." He tried smoothing her hair away from her face.

She slapped at his hand. "And why are you here?"

"You're in danger."

"I wasn't before you showed up."

Josh liked the way her lips puckered into a sexy pout. Charles really didn't do her justice when he described her.

"Chantelle, do you know what's going to happen next?"

Her eyes were wide for only a moment before they clouded over with distrust. "Sure. You're going to crawl out of here beaten and broken," she said dryly.

Josh shook his head and again reached for her face. When she raised her hand to block his touch, he grabbed her wrist and brought her fingers to his mouth. Instantly she straightened her fingers, letting her claws grow.

"Ignoring it doesn't mean it will go away," he explained. "I saw you reading the announcement on PI. This time that website actually announced something true. And believe me, I wish it was a preposterous lie as much as you do. But it's not. And you're on the list."

"You're lying." She wouldn't look at his face, instead focused on the hand he held between them. "And if you're going to try and throw nonsense at me to explain why you broke into my home, destroyed my lock, then you must think I'm a real stupid bitch."

"I know you're not stupid, Chantelle."

"Would you quit calling me that?" she hissed, finally meeting his gaze with green eyes that were so bright they glowed with confusion and worry.

"You don't want me to call you by your name?"

"My name is Chan." She relaxed slightly, searching his face. "Only my litter calls me Chantelle," she added quietly, admission enough that she believed he was sent by her litter.

"Why Shan?"

"It's short for Chantelle. C. H. A. N. Chan," she said.

"I see. You're still Drap, right? You haven't changed your last name and disowned your litter, have you?"

"Of course not." She scowled at him. "Which is why I know he didn't send you. My litter would call me if he was sending someone my way."

He noted that it wasn't easy to smell her lies. Charles didn't know how to reach Chantelle—Chan—because she hadn't been in touch with him in several years. Once Josh knew she was in Seattle, it wasn't too hard to sniff her out. Most leopards didn't like large cities. Chan hid herself easily by surrounding herself by humans. And he understood why she hid.

"Maybe you should call your littermate." He stood, holding on to her wrist and pulling her up with him. "Feed me your meat and talk to your littermate. We don't have a lot of time though."

He let go of her and she stalked into the kitchen. Her jeans fit snug around her short, slender legs. For a petite thing, she had one hell of a nice ass. And her soft golden hair, which fell in different lengths past her shoulders, dried slowly from the rain and looked tousled. As if she'd just enjoyed some rough sex.

And he didn't miss how fighting with him turned her on. Her scent became sweeter, muskier when her anger mixed with lust. Definitely something to remember.

Chan plopped down in her kitchen chair, picked up her plate of meat and put it on the other side of her laptop away from him, and then clicked her mouse, her extended nails clicking against the plastic.

Josh enjoyed an aggressive female. Passive, docile ones did nothing for him.

"I'm sure many won't believe the announcement posted is valid," he began, touching her shoulder as she stared at the main PI page. "It's probably just as well. The only ones who need to worry about this are those of us affected. The rest will continue to live their lives."

"I have a life," she hissed, stiffening under his touch.

Josh grabbed her hair. It was so smooth, like silk, thick and long. She gasped when he yanked her head back, looked up at him. The way she sucked in a harsh breath and her milky green eyes turned bright with a fiery glow, offered even more insight into her nature. Knowing that touching her, forcing her to adhere to him, made her hot even though she growled compelled him to push and see what else he could learn about her.

"And you're going to continue to have that life, which is why I'm here." He leaned over her, pulling harder until she looked at him upside-down. "I smell your intelligence, so I know you'll understand very soon that trusting me is in your favor. But, Chan, I also smell your lust. And I must admit, fighting with you turns me on too."

Dear Lord, she actually blushed. He didn't expect to gain this insight. Her hard edge, her willingness to attack first and ask questions later, was a façade. Chan wasn't the tough bitch she wanted him to see. He gazed past her chin and down her body at her exposed cleavage. Stretched before him, her nipples so hard they practically poked through her shirt, the view surpassed perfection. His hands itched to reach out and cup her fleshy mounds.

"Let me go so I can read this," she said, her voice quiet, almost placid.

Josh smiled. She was smart. He just told her that her aggressive nature made him hard, so she would now play the demure female. He doubted she would hold up the charade for long.

"By all means." He quit pulling her hair but kept his fingers tangled in it when she lifted her head and focused on her laptop.

Reaching over her shoulder, he leaned into her and picked up one of the slabs of meat. His adrenaline was maxed out since he'd spent the past few days sniffing her out. Once he found Chan's apartment, he staked the place out most of the day, waiting for her to come home. Keeping his nose to the ground and making sure Pard didn't send anyone else after her meant staying alert at all times. He didn't realize until he brought the steak to his mouth how hungry he was.

"Do you have to flaunt how despicable of a rogue you are?" she said with disgust. "It's a standard kitchen, the least you can do is find a plate and silverware."

Josh grinned, releasing her. Chan had just welcomed him into her den. He knew his satisfied scent reached her nose when he turned around from her counter, plate and fork in hand. She scowled at him before turning her angry glare toward her screen.

"You aren't sleeping here," she hissed.

"Then neither are you."

"No one is ever putting a collar on me," she whispered, her anger growing spicier by the moment. "This is bullshit." She slapped the table with her flat hand, making the plate with the rest of her meat on it rattle. "And you've seen this list of who they claim possesses some kind of strange voodoo or magic?"

"I have, and it's not voodoo. It's not magic." Josh stabbed the steak with his fork and then lifted it from the plate. "Leo

27

Pard wants to sniff out and cage all of us who are strong enough to be a threat to him. If he smells your fear, he'll keep that collar on you forever."

"You're insane." She watched him rip the meat with his teeth and then chew it. "There's no proof leopards possess the ability to see into the future. Just like there's no proof there is a male named Leo who leads those leopards possessing that gift."

"He doesn't lead them, he uses them."

Chan nodded once, her attention still on the screen, although now her expression and her emotions were in check. He didn't smell anything from her.

"This is all very interesting," she said, her tone too calm. "And I'm sure your intentions in seeking me out were in the best of interests. Leave your number and I'll give you a call."

She didn't look up at him. And he doubted she believed he would just saunter out of her home, especially now that she'd officially welcomed him inside.

Josh finished off the steak, which left his stomach grumbling for more food, and watched her while she intentionally didn't look at him and focused on her computer. Since she honored him by allowing him in her home, even if it was with the small gesture of telling him to find his own plate, he would treat it with respect. He turned and rinsed the dish and then opened her dishwasher, determined with a quick sniff that the dishes inside were dirty and placed the plate and fork inside. He closed the appliance just as Chan darted out her kitchen.

He raced out of the room and leapt over her coffee table, grabbing her before she could open her front door. "It's not going to work like this," he whispered into her hair, flipping her around. "Whatever it takes, you're going to learn I'm not your enemy."

She breathed heavily, staring up at him with that wild look once again in her eyes. "Tell me why you're really here," she whispered, a hint of fear mixing with her anger.

"I came for you." He leaned into her. "Because he wants you and he wants me. And he's not going to get either one of us."

She stiffened, which made her breasts swell against his chest and her nipples tease him ruthlessly. When she turned her head away from him, he grabbed her chin, adjusting her face to his, and then pressed his lips to hers.

She growled, shifting as if she would try fighting him again. But when he nipped at her lip and she opened to him, he impaled her with his tongue. Chan cried out into his mouth and dug her nails into his shoulders. Every inch of him hardened and all blood flowed quickly to his cock. He would have picked her up, tossed her back onto the couch and ripped her clothes from her body, except for one thing.

The moment he tasted her he knew without a doubt that her visions were as strong as his. Chantelle—Chan—saw the future, and probably on a regular basis. He wondered if she'd already seen him in her mind as he'd seen her. If so, maybe she submitted to him now because she already knew—the first time she saw him in the hallway—that they would end up fucking each other's brains out. There wasn't time to ask her about it right now. Leo Pard would destroy her while using her to learn more about the future. Which put her life in serious danger.

Chapter Three

&

Inviting a single male into her home was a stupid move. He would attack. She would kick his ass. One of them would die, or they would end up fucking.

Neither was on her agenda of things to do for the evening.

She tried not thinking about how his muscular body felt pressed against hers. Instead she tried dwelling on the uncomfortable wooden door behind her and how it pissed her off to be shoved up against it.

Feeling his hand in her hair, the other cupping her face and tilting her so he could deepen the kiss created sparks of desire inside her that continually ignited and exploded. But the worst of it, the hardest part to ignore, was how he tasted, how hot his mouth was as he moved over hers, and what a damned good kisser he was.

When she tried forcing her head to the side and breaking the kiss, his fingers pushed against her jaw bone, pinning her head in place. He tilted his, diving deep into her mouth with a tongue that possessed skills she'd never dreamed of.

Chan would not let his aggressiveness turn her on. It pissed her off, damn it. As if he had any right to demand anything from her. Something bad was about to happen—worse than bad, life-threatening. And this single male, this untamed rogue, wasn't going to make matters worse by fogging her brain and making her doubt her self-control.

She ran her hand up his arm, tracing her fingernails over the well-defined muscles in his biceps. He made a feast out of her mouth, exploring and challenging her while holding her jaw firm in his grip. Chan detected the change in his breathing when she continued dragging her fingernails, which were just slightly extended, over his shoulder and then to his neck. A powerful pulse throbbed against her finger when she touched his jugular.

He growled and pressed his body against hers, keeping her trapped and allowing her to feel how aroused he was. More than likely to the point where reasoning was no longer an option. Chan had taken out more than her fair share of humans who thought they might get a piece of tail off her. She didn't fool herself into thinking Josh would be as easy to conquer though.

Not to mention, he didn't feel or act anything like a human. No human male would ever attack her and consider it foreplay. Josh would throw her across the room without thought if she gave him any sign she wanted to get rough again.

And she didn't. But Chan wouldn't let him fuck her just because he wanted to. She dragged her fingers through his hair. His thick waves tumbled over her hand and wrapped around her fingers. She was overly aware of his rich aroma releasing in the air. It was a musky, intoxicating scent, thick with the power to make her crave him.

If she gave in to it.

Josh's mating scent, the smell he would release onto her if she were to allow him to come inside her, would seep through her pores for days, marking her and telling any other single male to keep his paws off. If she were to focus her attention more toward the smells in the air, she would be able to distinguish her scent from his. Because in the end, it would be the aroma she left on him that would remain stronger, bind him to her, and begin the taming process of turning him from a rogue into a male who would remain by her side.

Chan fought to keep her attention on other matters. His thick hair was smooth, long enough to grab hold of and sexy as hell when tousled. She dragged her hand up his body for a reason though, and it was that plan that needed to be foremost on her mind.

She untangled her fingers from his hair, knowing she needed to make her move now, before he made it impossible for her to catch her breath.

He bit her lip, surprising her for a moment into suspecting that he might know her plan. But it was his arousal, his warning that he was about to take their foreplay to the next level. Well, she was too.

Josh's hand moved and he grunted when he gripped her breast, squeezing and sending waves of lust rippling through her. She moved her hand, forcing herself to think about what she read on the Internet. He tweaked her nipple through her shirt and currents of electricity shot down her middle straight to her pussy.

Chan gasped, unable to stop herself as need burst to life inside her and moisture soaked her pussy. God damn him. He wouldn't seduce her. No way in hell would he saunter into her world, straight into her living room, and overpower and fuck her.

She focused on the PI website, on the announcement that might possibly steal away her freedom. There were some who could predict the future, who saw what other leopards couldn't. She'd heard about them all her life. But no one knew she was one of them—no one. Somehow her name had gotten on that list. She didn't know how—yet. What she did know was she wouldn't change how she lived for anyone, not even a hot, sexy rogue who claimed he was here to protect her.

She let her hand slide away from his head, pulling it back slowly. For a moment she saw Josh collapsed on her living room floor. He lay there, not moving while she breathed heavily and stared down at him. His hair fell over part of his face and one hand curled close to his chest. Chan recognized her living room floor. Josh wore the clothes he had on right now. But he was on the floor, as if he were dead.

However, he wasn't on the floor but pressed against her, his mouth finally leaving hers and creating moist trails across her cheek while his hand moved from her jaw to her neck. A vision. It was simply a vision. She had them all the time. Usually she could keep her wits about her, her scent unnoticeable, although around humans she didn't have to worry about that part, and prevent anyone from knowing she saw something they didn't. Had someone watched her closer than she thought? Somehow, did someone discover she was different?

Chan almost hesitated, fighting the quick surge of panic that Josh might already have the upper hand on her. But he didn't. And he never would. If she focused on kissing him, his touching her, the surge of panic wouldn't seed the air with its foul stench. All she smelled was the thick, sweet aroma from lust. Which was good. Just fine.

Chan drew her hand back, made a fist, and then pounded the side of his head with all her might.

"Take that!" she screamed.

She jumped to the side, needing the moment of surprise to create distance and prevent him from taking her down too when he fell.

Josh howled and staggered backward. Chan jumped in the air and kicked hard, pushing his body backward and sending him tumbling over her coffee table. He lay sprawled over her living room floor, rolled to his side and didn't move.

Just like the image in her head she saw moments before. God, she hated it when that happened.

Hurrying around him to her bedroom, Chan grabbed her backpack and stuffed a few items of clothing in it. She darted into her kitchen and shut down her laptop then downed her beer while the computer closed all programs.

"Come on, come on," she whispered, continually glancing into the other room where Josh remained on the floor. She didn't quite believe she could render a male leopard unconscious. Any moment now he would jump to his feet and grab her.

As she stared at him, her mind conjured a picture of him doing just that. Her being able to see a few seconds to a few minutes into the future wasn't a blessing. Usually it was annoying as hell. But it was also too much of a damned coincidence that Josh showed up saying he was here to protect her at the same time a new item posted on PI stating leopards who could see into the future were being gathered for training. As if seeing what would happen in the near future made her better than someone else. It wasn't as though she could change the future, or make the present a safer place with her knowledge.

Her laptop screen went black and she closed it quickly, slid it into her backpack with her clothes and then made a wide circle around Josh as she hurried to her door. Her boots were wet. She hated putting on wet shoes.

"Deal with it," she growled quietly, and grabbed her coat.

Adjusting her backpack strap over her shoulder, Chan opened her front door and then froze. Another image popped into her head. More males climbed the stairs in her apartment building.

The image disappeared.

"Is there another way out of here?" Josh asked from behind her.

"Crap!" Chan shrieked, practically jumping out of her skin. She turned around so quickly that the weight of her backpack almost made her stumble sideways.

"Would you rather fight those males on your own?" he asked quietly, standing in the middle of her living room and looking very unharmed.

"You faked getting knocked out," she accused.

He shrugged, the corner of his mouth twitching into what might be a smile. But he nodded toward the door. "Get ready to fight, or come up with another way out of here."

Chan could hear the males ascending the stairs, coming closer. She shut her door and then cursed when she couldn't lock it. There wasn't time to point out that Josh was an idiot for breaking her lock. And even if he had faked being knocked out, she'd kicked his ass—and that was twice now.

She ran into her bedroom and shoved open her blinds. Josh was right by her side when she grabbed the bottom of the window frame and pushed upward. The two of them were able to slide it open easily. Cold, wet air slapped Chan in the face as she straddled the window and then looked below her. A two-story fall was a bitch. She might not be human, but that didn't make her invincible.

"I don't know if this will hold you," she said, pushing away from the window and grabbing the drain pipe that went down the side of the building.

It was wet and cold and slippery. Chan didn't look up to see if he followed but held on, sliding down the side of the building fast. She hit the ground with a cruel thud. Then jumped out of the way. Josh flew down the pipe and landed seconds after she did. He took her hand and started running, obviously already knowing where he planned to go once they were out of her complex.

It should bother her that the town she'd come to know as home didn't bat an eye when two people raced, hand in hand, down the street. Humans were funny like that though. Not that she could brag much about leopards. Her kind didn't run in packs and didn't care about anyone usually other than their own litter.

Josh stood a good six inches taller than she did, and his long legs made it hard to keep up. He held on to her hand firmly though, barely slowing at intersections as they raced through her neighborhood into a commercial district and then farther into the city.

"I don't think we're being followed," she yelled at him, her backpack making her numb as it continually slapped against her while she kept pace.

"Not right now." Josh glanced down at her, his hair curling in the heavy mist and clinging to his forehead. "We can slow down," he said, and quit running. Then without asking, he slipped her backpack off her shoulder and flung it over his. "Are you okay?"

"Just peachy. Where the hell are we going?"

"To a friend's house. It's not much farther."

He didn't fight her when she slipped her hand out of his. Immediately, she missed the warmth that wrapped around her palm and shoved her hands into her coat pockets. Josh didn't wear a coat and his T-shirt clung to him like a second skin. His hair looked darker when it was wet and his expression was no longer seductive but all business. It gave him a hard edge, his high cheekbones and straight nose throwing in a distracting sex appeal.

"Let me guess. They're expecting us." She bet Josh planned to bring her to this "friend's house" all along. "Who is this friend?"

"No. He isn't expecting us. And you don't know him."

"You're sure about that?"

Josh looked down at her. His smile wasn't warm though, more like challenging. Heat traveled over her too quickly and she looked ahead of them, focusing on the road.

"You haven't spoken to your littermate in three years. And you aren't friends with anyone here in Seattle."

Chan scowled. He made it sound as if there were something wrong with her. And there wasn't. Humans were okay to work alongside, but they weren't exactly a species she would become bosom bodies with. And until tonight, she would swear there weren't any leopards in town.

"How do you know Charles?" she asked, deciding not to go in the direction of who she did and didn't know.

"He's mated to my littermate."

She remembered him telling her that in her kitchen and didn't know Charles had mated. Crap. Looking up at Josh quickly, he grinned at her surprised expression.

"He would have come up here to get you himself, I'm sure. But Jenny will be birthing their first litter very soon."

Chan exhaled. A pang of guilt crawled through her. Her only surviving littermate was about to sire his own litter. Granted they weren't the tightest litter around, but to hear such personal news from a stranger. Although, if what Josh said were the truth, he wasn't exactly a stranger. In fact, they were almost related.

* * * * *

When they walked up to an old home in the countryside outside Seattle, Chan shook her head. "We could have gotten here a lot sooner if we'd taken a more direct route. Do you really think we're safer walking in a zigzag pattern than we are arriving at this so-called sanctuary of yours?"

"It's only a sanctuary if it's not compromised." The rogue in her apartment was gone. The male who now walked in front of her, as if indifferent whether she followed or not, moved with a deadly, confident gait. Even his tone was deeper, darker, instead of flirtatious and seductive. They reached the door and he turned, looking down at her. "Don't speak unless someone directly asks you a question," he said quietly, and then ran his hand down the side of her hair, petting her. "Stay close and keep your emotions in check. You'll be safe with me."

What the hell? "This hardly sounds like a sanctuary if I have to watch my every move," she muttered. "Especially if you're the one I'm safe with."

Josh shook his head and then tapped her nose with his finger as if she were just a cub. "Bitch later. Be quiet now. Remember, emotions in check. You want to know something, ask me when we're alone."

He turned around and opened the door without knocking. Something flew before Chan, coming at her, its wingspan so intense that it blocked her view of everything around her. She almost ducked, grabbing her head with her hands, when she realized it was just in her head. Checking herself quickly, she ran her hand over her hair, not wanting anyone to catch her making a fool out of herself by hitting the ground and covering her head over something that wasn't really there.

"You're back already, Bard?" A large leopard male, probably somewhere around thirty, appeared in the foyer. "Is this her?"

"Nope. Her litter showed up minutes before I got there. Sounds like you should have gotten her, Race, and not me." Josh walked into the entryway and past the large leopard. He moved through the living room as if it were his own den, heading for a stocked bar and pulling open a small refrigerator. He turned and looked at Chan. "Beer?"

Since he pulled out two bottles and made quick work of twisting the lids off with his teeth, she nodded once and walked through the very spacious living area, aware of too many eyes watching her.

"Well then, who do we have here?" a tall, slender male leaning in the far doorway asked. The room seemed to silence, as if the rest of them didn't notice him standing there, or possibly because they all wanted to know who she was.

She would have introduced herself, but Josh spoke before she could, handing her beer to her while he began introductions.

"Jin is with me," Josh told him. "She just got here in town so I thought I'd bring her over. We'll work together to bring everyone else in."

She was glad she had her back to Josh and already took a sip of her beer. Otherwise she might have spit it all over him. Instead she leaned against the counter of the wet bar, adjusting herself so she stared at his profile. Josh spoke directly to the male leaning in the doorway.

"So you know each other well?" Race sauntered into the middle of the living room. He looked her over, making his message clear. If she was single, he would fight for the right to have her tonight.

Again she couldn't speak before Josh did, and remembered almost too late he'd said she should remain quiet unless someone directed a question at her. Already it was clear he knew this odd group pretty well. She didn't smell any other leopards in the room other than herself, Josh and the male coming at her.

"We've known each other a long time." Josh grabbed Chan and pushed her behind him just as the male came too close. "And she's here with me."

"We accept that." The male standing in the doorway pushed himself away and walked into the room. He gave the male leopard a piercing look with his cold gray eyes and the male scowled but backed off. "Jin," he said. "Have you had contact with Leo?"

Chan stared at his cold gray eyes. He was a tall, thin man with straight hair that was the same color as his eyes. An oversized T-shirt hung over his frame and his jeans were loose, adding to his gaunt look. But when he looked past her at Josh, and his eyes blinked, she suddenly understood the image that came to her when she'd walked into the house. The man before her was an owl.

"We haven't met," she said softly, understanding now why Josh told her to keep her emotions in check. Although she'd never met an owl before, she'd heard how good they were at detecting even the slightest negative emotion. There was some serious bullshit being shoveled around in this room, but until she understood what the hell was going on, she wasn't going to answer anyone's questions.

"Most everyone calls me Birdie. Welcome to my nest."

A female almost as tall as Birdie appeared in the doorway. "Better tell her the rules, seeing's she'll probably be the cause of most of our trouble now that she's here."

"Penny, she won't be any trouble. We're grateful for you taking us in," Josh said, his expression softening drastically when he spoke to the female owl.

"All are welcome here as long as there isn't any fighting. You want to tear each other up, you take it off my property. Any fighting, and you're banned from our nest." Birdie's tone was soft, soothing almost, but held a firmness to it that wouldn't allow argument. "Penny is the only one in the kitchen, unless invited. That's her food in there and she'll prepare it when she sees fit. You want to eat, you ask, or bring your own meat."

Birdie quit looking at her with those intense gray eyes and walked over to his mate. She whispered something to him and he nodded then turned around to face them again.

"We've got youngens. So if you're going to make a lot of noise when you fuck, you start early. I'm old and wise and know if my Penny has to listen to you howling all night long, she's going to want some from me. That's going to make me wake up grouchy, and I'll ban you from here faster than if you start a fight."

Race grunted, but then rubbed his hand over his mouth and looked at the floor.

"Understood." Josh took Chan's free hand and guided her away from the bar. "We'll see all of you tomorrow."

Chapter Four

ॐ

Josh pushed Chan up the stairs. "Don't say a word," he growled, sensing her growing outrage.

She stopped at the landing before the staircase turned and led to the second floor. Her green eyes sparked with anger. "You've got a hell of a lot of explaining to do," she hissed.

"Stifle that anger before someone smells it." He pushed her toward the rest of the stairs. "Trust me, if you want to live—and remain free—get your cute little ass up to our room."

"Our room?" she challenged defiantly.

The front door burst open downstairs and cold, damp air immediately filled the foyer and crept up toward Josh. Several leopards bounded into Birdie's nest and a mixture of emotions entered with them. His hand on Chan's backside, keeping her out of view in the stairwell, he turned to look down the stairs at the males and females filling the foyer.

"Birdie!" Tore Mann stood in the middle of the entryway, his large frame dwarfing the other males and females around him. "Birdie!" he howled again.

Josh doubted any other species could barge into this nest and howl as loud as Tore did and get away with it.

Birdie entered the foyer, actually standing taller than Tore but his thin frame making him look insignificant next to the male leopard.

"You're going to piss off Penny," Birdie said in his usual quiet tone.

"I'll make it up to her." Tore still growled with his deep baritone, but knowing the male as Josh did, he meant it and would probably suck up to the female bird when no one was looking. "There's six of us tonight. A lot of them have questions. I'd be eternally grateful if we could set up a meeting room."

Penny pushed her way around Birdie, rubbing her chin as she looked at the leopards filling her foyer. "What do we have here?" she asked, her voice exceptionally calm and soothing, which meant she was perturbed.

"Penny, how do you look so good after hatching a few young ones?" Tore purred.

Birdie's expression didn't change. He and Tore went back further than Josh knew either one of them. Penny clucked her tongue, shaking her head, although the compliment affected her. Tore could usually soothe any disgruntled female, which was one of the qualities that made him a good hunter.

"Why did you bring us to an owl's home?" one of the males standing just inside the front door asked. "You told me my special powers were needed, but why should I help owls?"

Penny stood at least as tall as some of the males she pushed around as she walked up to the male who just spoke. In spite of the fact even the females probably outweighed her, she didn't cower or hesitate as she hurried to the male and then poked his chest with her finger.

"If you have the gift I'm hearing about, or even if you had been brought up to display manners in your litter, you would know not to question anyone who opens their nest to you." She turned her back on him, crossing her arm and standing inches in front of him. "All of your leopards are welcome in my nest except for this male. My nest won't be disrupted by rudeness from any species."

The room grew quiet and Josh wished Chan wouldn't push her way out of the stairwell to witness the confrontation occurring below. If Tore figured out who she was, Josh would have explaining he would rather do when there wasn't a crowd surrounding them. He blocked her but sensed quickly that if he put his hands on her right now, she would make a scene.

Tore looked at the male at the door. "Leave now. You're on your own. Good hunting."

The male was ready to protest. He looked over Penny's head and then glanced down at her. Penny didn't turn around. Her lips were pressed into a thin line and she crossed her arms over her small breasts, taking her time looking at the other leopards. The room remained silent when the male finally turned and left the house.

"Bring everyone into the living room," Birdie said calmly. "Penny will fix food for anyone who's hungry."

Penny didn't question Birdie's announcement but walked quietly around the leopards and disappeared into the other room. Tore gestured to the group and the males and females shuffled into the living area. Tore glanced up the stairs at Josh.

"Did you get her?" he asked quietly.

Josh didn't mind lying to Tore. "Not yet. I'll talk to you after your meeting. You going to let that male get away?"

Tore didn't question why Josh wouldn't be joining them. The males and females demanded his attention. "Not your problem, Bard, is it?"

Josh grunted and turned away from the male, pushing Chan farther up the stairs and out of sight—and smell.

"He was asking about me," Chan whispered.

"Upstairs." Josh held on to her when they reached the top of the stairs and walked down the carpeted hallway. He paused in front of the room he'd been staying in for the past few days and put his hand on the doorknob. An image appeared in his mind. He saw Chan underneath him, her full breasts so perfectly round and bouncing as he drove into her repeatedly. Her nipples were large and hard and made his mouth water while she panted and reached for him.

"I'm not going in there," Chan announced, backing away from the door.

The stubborn look on her face belied the nervousness he suddenly smelled on her.

"Did you just see what's going to happen when we go in there?" he asked.

The way she looked up at him, her eyes widening and her lips parting, answered his question. Color flushed her cheeks at the same time her scent changed to something muskier. As quickly as she revealed the truth to him, her face hardened with anger and she put her hands on her hips, glaring at him.

"Why are you lying?" she demanded. "You denied you brought me here to that owl, and that leopard downstairs asked about me. You told him you didn't get me. Why does everyone want to know if I'm here? And who are you? What are hunters? You've lied to me from the beginning, haven't you? I bet you don't even know Charles."

"And it sucks that you don't have his phone number, doesn't it?" He wouldn't tell her how bad Charles felt when he realized he didn't know his littermate's number or address. All he had was the city, and the rest was left up to Josh.

"I want answers—now," she demanded.

Josh turned and opened the door to his room. He grabbed Chan when she tried walking down the hallway. She howled and scratched when he threw her over his shoulder and headed into his room. Kicking the door closed with his foot, he held on to her while she violently tried attacking him.

Carrying her across the room, he peeled her off his shoulder, yanking her coat off and dropping it to the floor. With her claws and teeth extended, he threw her onto the bed.

She jumped right back at him. "You lie to me and you don't have manners," she growled. "You give rogue males a bad name."

Josh grabbed her arms and pushed her onto the bed, forcing her to her back and pinning her wrists to either side of her head. "You've got a lot of misconceptions rushing around in that pretty head of yours." He pushed his hips between her legs and came down on top of her. "Let me straighten one of them up for you right now. Females don't beat their males into submission. Males conquer the female, and with some females, I'm starting to think that might include using a leash and collar."

"Why you..." She brought her legs up and he smiled down at her outraged expression, keeping her trapped and unable to move. She exhaled loudly and turned her head, refusing to look at him. A strand of her hair fell across her face. "I've lived here for three years peacefully with no one giving me any grief. What have I done wrong that you suddenly rip that life from me?"

"You haven't done anything wrong, Chan," he told her.

"Yes I have," she hissed. "I came home from work instead of going for a beer. I should have gone somewhere else so I wouldn't have met you."

Josh let go of one of her wrists and reached for his phone. Chan twisted underneath him and pushed her hand against his chest, her nails still slightly extended. "If you think you can force me to do anything, then you better think again. I can kick your ass, and it wouldn't be to tame you, or to make you mine. You aren't worth it!"

He let her howl at him and pulled his phone off his belt, held it up before her face. "Call your littermate," he said quietly. "His number is in this phone." He flipped it open and handed it to her. "Go ahead," he prompted. "You're going to get your hot little ass killed if you keep howling and hissing. I can beat you into submission, or give you what you need to satisfy you that I'm on your side."

He doubted Chan cried much. Her green eyes rimmed with moisture though when she ripped the cell phone from his hand. She scrolled through his address book. "You don't have that many friends," she said stiffly.

"Us rogue males don't have a lot of use for cell phones," he offered, searching her face for any sign she might be calming down. "Besides, there are very few leopards who I would trust with my number."

She glanced up at him. "Charles' number isn't on your list."

He nodded to the phone. "Jenny. My littermate is Jenny. Charles is her mate."

She stared at the phone again and then pushed the buttons until he heard it ringing when she put it up to her ear. "Hello, yes." She cleared her voice. "I want to speak to Charles."

Josh pushed the hair from her face as his littermate demanded to know who called.

"This is Chan. Chantelle. I'm his littermate."

She didn't look at him when there was silence on the other end of the line.

"Chantelle?" Charles' baritone boomed through the phone.

Chan bit her lip. "Hey, Charlie. It's me, Chan."

"You're calling on Josh's phone?"

"He's sitting on top of me." She bit her lip to keep from smiling when Charles growled at the other end of the line. "What's going on, Charlie? Why did you send him to me?"

"I sent him because I trusted him, but if he's hurting you…"

"He's not going to hurt me," she said, shooting Josh a glance that easily could be interpreted as a warning glare. "But why did you send him? What's going on?"

"The hunters were given a list. Your name was on it. Josh was the only one who could come get you and keep you alive through this nightmare."

"List? What are you talking about? What are hunters?"

"Let me talk to Josh."

Chan growled and pushed her lower lip out in a sensual pout as she thrust the phone at him.

"Your littermate doesn't like being left in the dark," Josh said, adjusting his weight so he wouldn't hurt her and then leaning closer so they could both hear Charles.

"I don't care how stubborn she's being. She's alive and for that I'm grateful."

Josh watched Chan look down his body, hooding her gaze from him with her long, thick lashes.

"We're staying at a sanctuary right now, neutral to all species." Josh leaned on his elbow but kept his leg draped over her body. With his free hand he stroked her flesh just above the collar of her shirt. "Birdie is an old friend of mine. But he and his mate will welcome any species as long as their rules are honored. Tore is using this sanctuary and Race is too. So I'm getting a good idea of how many are coming in on the list."

"What about Leo? Have you heard from him?"

At the mention of Leo's name Chan looked at him, shocked.

"No. But I'm sure I will soon. I told everyone here that I don't have Chan yet. They all think she's another hunter. Apparently Leo already doesn't trust me to bring her in or he wants her pretty badly. We got out of her apartment just as two males arrived. My guess is Leo sent backup."

"Josh. Protect my littermate. We're all that's left and if she dies…"

"She won't die. You have my word."

"Your word is good enough for me. Keep me posted."

"Good hunting."

"And good hunting to you both." Charles hung up.

Josh secured the phone to his belt and traced his finger down her neck again. She slapped at him and he grabbed her hand, bringing her fingers to his mouth.

"Are you satisfied I'm not lying to you?"

She tried pushing out from underneath his leg but he liked where she was. He grabbed her chin and forced her to look at him.

"You're still lying to everyone here though. How do I know you aren't deceiving Charles too?"

"He's mated to my littermate. I would kill for him." He was ready for her stubbornness to go away. And although he swore to himself over and over again he would never go through the hell that he'd watched so many of his friends experience when it came to taming a wild, untamed single female, he held her face and lowered his mouth over hers, stifling her further accusations.

Her growl turned to a whimper but she didn't relax, not completely. More than likely because she didn't trust him. Chan was intelligent, a strong, beautiful single female who'd managed to hold her own for several years now. Granted, living among humans made it easier for her to do so, but he credited her for her ability to protect herself.

Under normal circumstances.

If another hunter had found her before he did, her fighting skills wouldn't have helped. Any species who could be bought would be blindly loyal to Leo, without caring to know the inside details of why they hunted these particular leopards. Unfortunately, mercenaries were easy to hire. Josh preferred to understand his prey. There were five hunters in his species, hunters who hunted more than their kill, that is. Being a hunter was usually a generational trade. His sire was a hunter who retired from the dangerous lifestyle once he mated. It still got him killed. Even though Josh accepted the title of who and what he was, and sought out leopards who were a danger to their species, or other species, he didn't do it for the money. Hunters existed to keep leopards safe, protect them from each other and themselves. Josh was a hunter because he cared. "I could make a feast out of you," he whispered against her lips, loving how hot and sweet she tasted.

"If you're hungry, I'm sure Penny will prepare us food. I'll go ask her." Chan made an effort to get off the bed.

"I doubt anything she could make would appease my hunger." He ran his hand down her middle, feeling the swell of her breasts under his fingertips and the edge of his palm.

She quivered under his touch but then looked at him with sharp green eyes. "And you think I could satisfy that hunger?"

"For a while," he told her. "But then I would want more of you."

"I might disappoint you."

"You haven't so far."

Chan shifted under his leg, not trying to get up but instead making herself comfortable. She turned her head, causing her hair to fan out around her face. The look was beyond that of a skilled seductress and hardened every inch of him.

"Maybe I was wrong to attack you so brutally," she whispered, her voice a soft, alluring purr while her green eyes turned milky. "Obviously when I meant to protect my home and myself, you mistook it as a sign of sexual curiosity."

"Chan, you knew I wouldn't hurt you because I told you I wouldn't. Attacking turned you on. You love the fight. And, little cat, you are still very turned-on. I can smell your sweet cream on you. You are soaked right now, swollen and burning up inside, aching for me to enter you."

"What would Charles think if he knew you were trying so hard to fuck me right now?" she challenged, her gaze fogged with desire in spite of her effort to sound aloof and indifferent.

Josh smiled, running his fingers just underneath her shirt and over her soft flesh. "I watched him pursue my littermate for months, saw the scratches and bruises on both of them, and finally witnessed him taming her and then taking her as a mate." He looked up in time to see her open her mouth, ready to challenge his words even when she hadn't been there to see the events transpire. He added quickly, shaking his head, "Charles has no room to speak when it comes to how I treat you. He's got my word you'll be protected and won't get killed. Beyond that, he can't make any demands."

"So you traveled here to Seattle with the intention of seducing me to offer me protection? And you still haven't been very clear on what exactly I'm being protected from."

"I came here to take you before any of the other hunters could," he answered honestly. "But truth be told, Charles' description of you was slightly inaccurate."

"Oh really?"

"I'm afraid he sees you as rather plain and quiet."

Chan looked down, giving his words some thought. He pushed his hand under her shirt and lifted it as he moved to touch her. She hissed in a breath when he cupped her round breast and squeezed a nipple between two fingers.

When he lifted his leg off her and adjusted himself to a sitting position, she tried doing the same. Josh grabbed her shirt and pulled it up.

"So after knowing me for only a couple hours you feel you've accurately determined I would fuck you? I don't know anything about you, other than you know my littermate and you're a hunter, whatever the hell that is."

She refused to lift her arms so he bunched her shirt over her breasts. Flesh swelled over white silk and her nipples poked against the fabric. His mouth watered as he gazed at them, trying to decide if he should force her arms up, or simply tear the shirt from her body.

"There are five hunters alive right now. If a leopard endangers our species, we take care of him. If there is trouble that litters can't handle, we step in and fix it. My sire was a hunter before me, and now I follow in his footsteps. Leo Pard contacted all five of us and offered an incredibly large amount of money for us to bring his chosen leopards to him," he offered, keeping his gaze on her breasts.

He knew the information would send Chan over the edge. Like most leopards, she didn't believe in Leo Pard. It was easier to deny his existence than accept that someone walked among them with the power to control their lives. Also, like most leopards, she wouldn't know anything about hunters. They were a quiet group, doing what was necessary to ensure their species didn't die out.

"What?" she growled, her long, wavy hair falling over her exposed breasts when she leapt off the bed. "What kind of bullshit are you feeding me?"

He didn't let go of her shirt and the sound of the fabric tearing brought his blood to a boil. Chan stumbled toward him, unable to pull away in spite of her efforts with his grip on her shirt and her body still wearing it.

"Are you trying to tell me there is actually a leopard named Leo? And I've never heard of hunters before. Are you some kind of mercenary?" She shook her head violently, denying his answers before he even spoke them. "You're lying. I know you are."

"You just admitted not knowing me. And you know nothing about Leo Pard, including whether he exists or not. I doubt you're so unintelligent as to pass judgment with such few facts." He twisted her shirt in his fist, his knuckles buried between the swell of her breasts, and then yanked her to him.

She dug into his fist, fighting for him to release her, but then let go quickly when she fell forward. Her hands slapped the bed and she locked her arms, looking up at him while her hair flew wildly around her face and shoulders.

"What are you planning to do with me?" she hissed, barely moving her mouth and speaking through her teeth. Her eyes were burning with emotions. And in spite of her sudden anger, an emotion he was learning sprang forth easily in her, he still smelled her intense arousal. "Why did you lie to everyone about who I was? And no lies this time, Josh. Don't think you can seduce me without telling me the truth."

"Would you believe the truth?"

"Yes."

Already he understood that it was hard to smell lies on her. More than likely, it was because Chan convinced herself that she wasn't lying. She didn't trust him and therefore wasn't sure she would believe anything he said. He much preferred the rich aroma that smelled sweeter than syrup when she was turned-on. Even as she glared at him, searching his face and ready to pounce on any discrepancy, he knew without doubt her pussy was covered with rich cream. And he couldn't wait to taste it. She might not trust him, but he doubted Chan trusted anyone. She would learn though—implicitly.

"I've never met Leo Pard. If he is one male, or an organization using the cover of an urban legend, I can't say. Nor can any of the other four hunters." He pulled harder on her shirt, forcing her closer. When she almost fell on him, scratching his legs through his jeans in her effort to keep her distance, Josh let go of her shirt and grabbed under her arms, lifting her onto his lap. "We were e-mailed instructions. I saw your name on the list and knew Charles would want me to protect you. So I accepted the job so I could specifically bring you in. I know almost all of the hunters, but none of them would protect you like I can."

He adjusted her so she sat sideways against him and her soft ass pressing against his cock created a pressure inside him that demanded attention. Josh fought the urge to rip her clothes completely from her body. He would give her the information she wished to hear. Then he would fuck her.

"What are you supposed to do with me?" She twisted her body to face him and tried pulling her shirt down over her breasts.

He wrapped his fingers around her arm, keeping his touch gentle. When he wasn't aggressive, she stilled, looking down at his neck and not moving. He put her hand in her lap, keeping her breasts exposed, and then let go of her arm.

"In the e-mail there was a link to a website where we were told we should check in, submit any questions and get further instructions. When we picked up a leopard from the list, we checked them off on the website. At that time, we're given further instructions. Since I haven't checked you off of that list, and don't plan on doing so, I'm not sure what he would have me do with you."

"I see." She swallowed, glancing quickly at his face through her long lashes before looking down at her hands.

Just tonight she'd seen part of the instructions in action. He guessed she suspected that. She was calmer now and possibly would digest what he told her. He brushed her hair behind her shoulder and she didn't move. Although he seriously doubted she now showed him a docile side to her, more than likely she believed him. That was a step in the right direction.

"There are twenty names on that website, males and females around the country. With the others I've picked up, the instructions following were the same — bring them here to Birdie's sanctuary. I'm not sure yet where he plans on taking everyone, or the specifics concerning what he'll do with you exactly. What I do know is that I don't like it, and so in your case, intervened." He didn't add in his case as well.

He would learn how his name appeared on that list. No one knew what he saw — no one. Before tonight, he'd never implied to another leopard he could see things before they happened. Knowing Chan saw the future also made it seem natural to share what he saw. Nonetheless, his guard needed to remain high, even when it came to Chan. She was still too skittish to trust implicitly, and she didn't trust him.

"I don't understand why I would be on that list." She didn't deny her abilities to see things, but he guessed she believed she'd done a good job from keeping any other leopards from knowing her secret, as had he.

He touched her chin, lifting her face so she would look at him. She didn't fight him and stared at him with such sensual, beautiful eyes that for a moment he considered lying to her.

"We were told the list is ranked in order of importance of leopards who can see things others can't. From what I've learned, Leo Pard believes he can train these gifted leopards to understand their visions, know exactly when and where what they see will happen, and get to where they can even choose to see the future if they are told to do so."

She looked at him wide-eyed. "That's insane, complete bullshit. If something like that were possible, it would have been done by now."

When she tried jumping off him, he wrapped his arms around her, cradling her against him.

"Like I said, the leopards are numbered on the list, showing who is the most important to Leo due to the level of their gift."

"And he thinks I'm the one who sees the best visions?" she whispered, fear hitting too quickly for her to hide her scent from him.

He cuddled her closer. "Which is why everyone wanted to know if you were here yet. They are curious, but also envious. Some leopards brag about their ability to see the future."

He didn't need to explain how this put her in a dangerous position. She stilled to where he barely felt her heart beat, and didn't say anything. Nor did she try moving out of his arms.

The pain he saw in her eyes brought him to a decision quickly, one he prayed he wouldn't live to regret. "I'm on that list too. My name is number three."

"Who is number two?"

"Tore Mann. He showed up downstairs when we came up here. I don't want him to know you're here, or any of the other hunters, for that matter. All of them are very anxious to be the one to turn you over to Leo Pard."

"But there isn't anything special about me," she insisted, the smell of her lie faint but noticeable. "You make it sound as if we're magic like the Malta werewolves. And they were kicked out of their own country because they were different. Then they about destroyed themselves here."

He stroked her hair, running his hand down her arm and then turning her farther so her torso twisted and her large breasts almost spilled out of her bra. His comments scared her, but she wouldn't cower. What he knew about her already, Chan would be more inclined to leap into the middle of the problem and kick ass until she resolved it.

"Those werewolves weren't magic, but they possessed an ability to bend the elements to their will. That isn't what we're about. If I want to throw you across the room, I'm going to have to physically pick you up to send you flying. I can't do it with my mind. But there is something about us. How this Leo Pard knew it about you and me, or any of the others who didn't advertise it, I don't know—yet." He rubbed his thumb over her moist lips and his cock grew painfully hard. "Little cat," he whispered, his voice turning gravelly when his body hardened and a more carnal side of him threatened to surface. "Right before we walked into this room, you saw as well as I did what would happen after both of us were in here."

"Do you have some special sense that allows you to know if someone has a vision?" Her tone turned hard, almost hateful.

"No."

"I didn't think so."

"But I saw what we're going to do in this room." He gripped her neck, poising his thumb so she couldn't turn her head and forced her to look at him. "And I saw your face and smelled your reaction when I asked you about it. I don't need some special sense to understand your reaction when you see yourself in a vision, naked and coming very hard while I'm on top of you, buried deep inside you."

"I didn't see shit," she snapped, and for the first time the smell of her lie was apparent. She stubbornly lowered her eyes, refusing to look at him even though he held her face captive. "And furthermore, I won't have anything to do with a leopard who steals me from my home and intends to turn me over to someone he doesn't know simply because my name is on some fucking list."

She pressed her lips together, looking as if she were struggling not to pant. Her nipples were so hard they almost poked through the thin film of material covering them. The only smell stronger than her lie was the enticing scent of her lust.

"I'm glad to hear that," he said without hesitating. "That assures me you won't go to any of the other hunters. And I'll kill any of them who try taking you from me. I'm not releasing you to anyone. But the safest place for both of us to be right now is right in the heart of the action. It's always best to know what your enemies are going to do, without them knowing you know their plan."

"Then maybe I'm right where I'm supposed to be," she said slowly, her tone lowering to a sensual purr. "Since I'm still not convinced who is my real enemy."

Josh watched her eyes smolder as the smell of her desire filled the air around them. He ignored her implication that she didn't trust him. In spite of not smelling another lie, he guessed she trusted him more than she wanted him to know. Or she wouldn't be relaxing in his arms right now.

"We're going to find that out." He lowered his gaze to her breasts and brushed his finger over the swell just above her bra. "It will take patience, paying attention and not doing anything to alert the others that we have our own agenda."

She wrapped her fingers around his wrist but couldn't move his hand. He quickly allowed his claws to extend and swiped the small piece of material between her breasts. The bra split in two and her large breasts bounced free from the confinement and looked even fuller, rounder and perkier now that they were exposed.

"That was my only bra," she complained, looking down at his hand and then slowly up to his face. Her teeth pressed against her lips. "I'm not sure you and I have the same agenda."

"Chan, you're so aroused right now the smell of your lust is strong enough to get drunk off of." His claw wasn't completely returned to human form when he brushed it over her puckered nipple. "You're making me want you more and more every second."

Chan sucked in a sharp breath. "And temptation isn't something you can fight?"

"This temptation is stronger than most," he whispered, dragging his fingernail down her middle and then unbuttoning her jeans. "Wouldn't you agree, little cat?"

"Nothing is too strong to fight," she said, her voice husky. "And if you think fucking me will instill some kind of loyalty between us, you're wrong."

"So you just wish to fuck for pleasure?" He unzipped her jeans and then grabbed the denim at her waist. It took little effort to lift her. But with his cock swollen and throbbing against his jeans, it was a bit more strenuous to lift her in his arms and stand next to the bed. She slid down his body, her breasts pressing against his chest and proving to be even worse torture than waiting to fuck her. "Do you not care about there being a bond between you and the male you have sex with?"

"Loyalty comes with trust. And trust is earned, not bought with pleasure."

"Then for now we'll just enjoy the pleasure." He pulled down her jeans, knocking her off balance and pushing her facedown onto the bed as he peeled them down her legs.

She was trapped with her jeans wrapped around her boots and making it impossible for her to spread her legs.

When she kicked, the aroma of her cream dripped rich and thick in the air, filling his lungs and damn near pushing him beyond any limit of control. Flipping her over, he yanked off one boot and then the other. He tossed her jeans to the floor and then grabbed her ankles, spreading her open.

"Oh fuck," he growled, almost losing it over how fucking hot she was. It was all he could do not to rip her panties off her, but made quick work of taking them off too. "You're so beautiful, Chan."

She clutched her shirt, which was still balled up under her arms, and stared at him with a wild look in her eyes. Her long blonde curls were tousled around her head, making her appear even more the temptress. Josh knelt before her, sure he would drool like a starving cub in the next minute if he didn't taste her.

Holding on to her legs, he slid his hands up past her knees, keeping her open and taking in how perfect her pussy looked.

"I need to taste you," he told her, adjusting himself as he knelt against the bed and lowered his mouth to her smooth-shaven pussy.

"No," she said quickly, and then cried out, digging her nails into his scalp, trapping his head between her legs as he ran his tongue over her already-soaked entrance.

Chapter Five

ꙮ

"You want me to stop?" he asked.

"What did I say?" She dug her fingers into his thick hair, its coarseness tantalizing the sensations already rippling through her. "You don't listen." Damn him. She was practically panting.

"I'm paying very close attention. I promise." His baritone vibrated against her soaked pussy, sending shivers over her almost-naked body.

She would give him that. He was an expert with detail and was skilled with more than just the art of manipulation. His fingers pressed roughly into her flesh, and his extended nails scraped her body until he gripped her breasts. He tugged just enough to feed the fire already burning inside her.

Pleasure like this didn't exist. Chan wasn't a virgin. She knew sexual satisfaction. But this, what Josh did with his mouth, with his tongue, with his hands, was something in a category all by itself.

She let go of his hair and grabbed his hands, squeezing harder. Which was all the invitation he needed. He tugged on her breasts, pulling and becoming rough. Just the way she liked it. When his fingers grazed her nipples and then pinched, his lips puckered around her clit.

"Dear God!" she cried out, lashing her head from side to side.

Her mind was a spectrum of color, warm and then burning hot. Flashes of yellows and greens turned quickly into crimson and burgundies. Her lashes fluttered over her eyes, everything around her a blur as her world melted and drifted to a place she'd never been to before.

"Do you know how good you taste?" he asked, his lips moving over her clit and then closing in on it again, sucking harder.

She about bounced off the bed. "Damn it, Josh," she growled, wanting to lash out at him, to grab him and rake her claws over all of that hard muscle.

She wanted to feel him buried deep inside her. If he fucked her, the ache that throbbed out of control inside her would be appeased. All he needed to do was ram his cock into her pussy with the aggression she knew he possessed.

There were male leopards in her past, all of whom she met before coming to Seattle. It was consensual sex, each time taking place after a group run in their fur. Sloppy, sweaty, primal sex in their skin before parting ways and never seeing each other again. As much as she hated to admit it and would never voice to anyone, she'd never known true sexual satisfaction. In her opinion, males just weren't strong enough to conquer the need that brewed deep inside her womb. They were wild, yes. Out of control and quite often lacking manners, most definitely. But training them to please her the way she needed it was work she didn't want to waste her time on. Besides, training meant taming, taming led to mating, and the last thing she wanted was some docile, annoying male clinging to her for the rest of her life.

"You're almost there, little cat." He spoke with so much assurance, as if he knew her body better than she did. "Let go. Give it to me. I want all you have."

No one took all she had. Chan wouldn't allow it. That meant surrender, submitting wholly to another. Which would make her vulnerable. As often as she swore she would never tame a male, she would swear and howl even louder that no male would control her.

"No." She let go of his hands and grabbed her head, fighting to regain control of her body.

Tightening her legs, she would come, but she would remain in control. If she could only hold on, pace her body so she could gain her pleasure but not slip over the edge. Every inch of her stiffened. She focused on her thigh muscles and how his hair tickled her tender skin. Sensations rippled over her, causing the tiny hairs on her body to stand erect. It was as if he'd turned her body into one overexposed nerve ending, making her ultrasensitive to his touch, his breathing, his body brushing against hers.

"Oh yes, Chantelle," he purred. "You can't stop this. I can taste how close you are."

He thrust his tongue into her pussy and licked at her walls. When he growled, it filled her with smoldering energy that threatened to take over. She arched off the bed, coming to a sitting position, and tried grabbing his head.

His hands pressed against her abdomen while he continued devouring her. He milked her, taking more than she wanted to give him and ignoring her claim that she wouldn't let go.

"Shit. It's too much." She could feel the convulsions building inside her.

Josh reached up with one hand and pushed her back down on the bed. He held her pinned, his strength seeming to be ten times hers. She hated submitting, dreaded it worse than anything. Letting go, giving in to the pressure growing inside her, would be an admission of weakness.

"It's not enough," he told her, his mouth becoming gentle.

His lips and tongue stroked her soaked flesh. It felt good—so damned fucking good. She sank into the bed, covering her face with her hands and groaned loudly.

"That's it, baby. You're incredible. Do you know that? Absolutely fucking perfect."

Paying attention to his words distracted her. It's what he wanted, she told herself. If she focused on something else, on the situation that had just crashed into her, on him entering her life and stealing her from her home. Maybe if she yelled at herself for going with him instead of staying put and fighting for her home, for her way of life. Maybe if she did that she wouldn't feel the incredible throbbing that built inside her until there wasn't any more room for her to contain it.

Her thigh muscles started quivering. Every inch of her smoldered, threatening to break out into full-fledged flames in the next moment. He was fucking perfect. Better than perfect. Josh possessed skills that should be illegal and might very well be.

God. Maybe if she let go. The pressure was so great. The torment thrashing through her was too intense. It built, growing, expanding inside her until she swore it seeped from her pores. The smell of her orgasm filled the air a second before it erupted inside her.

"Damn you," she yelled. "I hate you!"

He pinched her breasts, pulling on them and sending streaks of fiery currents straight to her pussy. At that same time he lapped at her cunt, burying his face in her throbbing pussy and devouring her while her come soaked her thighs and ass.

"You don't hate me." His words sounded so far away, as if he were a mile off, watching and witnessing her fall over the edge.

But she wasn't alone. His hands were on her, stroking and touching as though he knew exactly where she needed to be caressed to help pull the orgasm out of her and relieve the out-of-control pressure.

Chan screamed and then bit down on her hand, thrashing her head from side to side and barely feeling the thick strands of hair clinging to her face. She couldn't stop coming and slipped over the edge, falling, falling while every inch of her turned into a fiery current of incredible passion. She clawed at the bed, at the air, at his body, raking her nails over his shoulders. The warm strength of his body against her fingertips made her ache to feel the rest of him.

Josh purred with intense male satisfaction, drinking in every bit of her, and then tenderly placed gentle kisses over her pussy, her inner thighs while his touch turned gentle.

It didn't occur to her that he'd moved or undressed. He no longer knelt but climbed onto the bed. And he was completely naked. With no effort, he lifted her into his arms and adjusted her body so she lay with her head on his chest, her body cradled next to his.

"Relax, little cat. I know you haven't experienced completely letting go before."

She tensed, pushing against him even as her body still quivered with the aftermath of her orgasm. Pressing her hand against his chest, she swore her body tingled with such severity that she could barely feel him.

"Don't pretend to know what I have or haven't experienced." She tried growling and hated how sated her voice sounded.

Josh turned, one arm underneath her neck, and ignored her comment. He pressed his fingers under her chin, silently demanding she look at him. She closed her eyes. The last thing she wanted was to see his gloating expression. It was enough to breathe in all of that male satisfaction until it filled her lungs. Let him think she surrendered and he was victorious. She would strike back when his ego was the most swollen, knocking him back down to a size she could handle. He wouldn't control her.

"Chantelle," he whispered, grabbing her attention by using her full name.

She opened her eyes and glared at him. "Don't call me that."

"Don't try to block me out," he said, and then stroked her cheek.

"I'm not." She inched away from him. Her body sizzled, and when he brushed against her, it made her swell with need all over again. Somehow she needed to regain control.

"You're fighting it. And don't tell me you didn't enjoy coming."

"Fine. I enjoyed it. I fucking came like I never have before. Are you happy now?"

She clawed at his chest when he lifted her up over him. "Stop it. Josh, no."

"No. You stop it." His tone was fierce and his expression darkened. "You're so damned scared of getting too close to anyone. Why the hell is that, Chan? Charles told me you'd be difficult, but he never suggested you had a fucking brick wall around you. Do you like being in a tight cage?"

"No," she spat, glaring down at him while her hair fell over her shoulders, limiting her vision so all she saw was his determined expression. "I'm not in some self-imposed fucking cage. Cut the crap. I'm not going to submit to you. Not now. Not ever."

"And you think letting go and coming is the same as submitting?" he asked incredulously.

"Look at how you're gloating."

He relaxed his grip on her and she found herself straddling his muscular body with his hard cock throbbing dangerously close to her soaked pussy. He was the one with incredible self-control. Who the hell was she fooling? He'd pulled her over the edge and she didn't stop him. What made matters even worse was that she wanted more, craved him inside her so desperately she could barely think.

As she scowled at his intense expression, willing her anger to surpass the need torturing her insides, a picture appeared before her eyes. She no longer saw Josh's face but herself, standing before him, leaning against him with her arms draped over his shoulders.

"I love you," she told him.

The image disappeared like a TV shutting off. Chan blinked, her nerves suddenly bound so tight she couldn't move.

"What?" he asked. "What did you see?"

"Nothing."

"Tell me."

She wanted to wrap her hands around his neck and shake him. "I don't have to tell you shit. You have no right to demand to know what's going on in my head."

"If you see anything that might help us, or prevent either of us from getting hurt, then I have a right to know," he said firmly.

What she saw definitely would cause one of them to get hurt—her. Falling in love with a rogue like Josh would destroy her. She didn't even know what side he ran on.

"I didn't see anything," she whispered, and grew irritated as his expression turned defiant. "Nothing. It was nothing. Okay?"

Josh nodded once, his face tight with control. "You're right." He gripped her arms, lifting her as if he would toss her to the side. "It's just about the pleasure. We already agreed to that."

She leaned, ready to catch herself when he threw her. But he didn't throw her, or even release her. Instead he moved her over him and then pulled her down with her legs still spread wide over his body. His cock impaled her so smoothly, gliding in as if it were home. She arched, clawing at him while she was filled as though the void inside her went clear up to her fucking bellybutton.

"God damn it," she cried out, shocked at how much her voice sounded like a growl.

With one thrust he took away her ability to control her actions, to do anything other than hold on and crave more of him. And he was quick to fulfill her desires. Even though she was on top, straddling him, Josh grabbed her waist and thrust up, controlling the moment.

She rode an untamed beast, one so savage and primal with his lustful needs that she barely possessed the strength to keep from falling off. Except he kept her pinned securely to him, bound by his strong hands wrapped around her waist.

His cock glided in and out of her, stretching inner muscles and stroking places inside she never knew could be so sensitive.

"You're fucking tight as hell," he growled, his scent mixing with hers so she couldn't tell them apart. His hooded gaze made it even harder to read his emotions.

For once it would be nice if the images she saw would benefit her in some way. Who the hell cared what happened five minutes from now, an hour from now, or even a fucking year from now? She wanted insight, anything to help her manipulate the situation back to her corner. Her vision just told her she would willingly hug this male and profess her love for him. And not once had any of her visions not come true. That didn't help her understand him now. She needed to know how to run from where she was at the moment to where she would be in that vision, and there weren't any clues to sniff out. All she knew right now was that she wanted control.

And at the same time she wanted to come. Damn him for making her feel like this. Lust rode her as hard as he did. And she couldn't catch up. He plunged into her pussy, reaching somewhere deep inside her where she was sure hadn't been touched before.

The instant he pressed against it with his cock, she exploded.

"Oh shit," she howled. There was no stopping it. No controlling it. She came in waves, convulsing over him.

"That's it, sweetheart. Your pussy is so tight around my cock. You feel so good," he purred, soothing her scorched brain with words that shouldn't make her feel better.

"It's just sex," she whimpered, hating the sound of her voice. And then instantly wanted to retract the words when she smelled her own lie. It sunk in the air around them and practically drowned out the sweet aroma of their combined arousal.

Chan managed to open her eyes and found him staring directly at her. When she tried lifting herself, he held her close, rolled them over, keeping them together until she lay flat with her head sinking into the pillows.

She brought her legs up, allowing him to go deeper. Josh thrust quickly without hesitating and filled her, stroking yet another part of her that he didn't touch with her on top.

He growled, keeping up the momentum, fucking her hard and fast while his skin started to glisten. She was sure she'd never seen a more beautiful sight. So many muscles bulged. His chest was tight, his body tense as if he would leap at any moment.

Unable to stop herself, although barely able to move with his cock pressing deeper, filling her, she traced the fine red lines she'd created on him when she'd scratched him earlier.

Josh looked down at her, his teeth extended and pressed against his lips. He was sexier than hell. His blond and red hair curled in thick waves, strands drifting over his forehead and falling past his ears.

She raked her fingertips down to his abdomen and then up his arms, loving the smooth warmth of his skin and the perfect contours of so many muscles. He growled and his cock swelled, pushing the pressure already engorging out of control inside her to a new level.

"Fuck me harder," she demanded. "Fuck me, Josh."

His body quivered where she touched him as he built speed, impaling her deeper and deeper, hitting that spot again and again until she exploded. An array of light flashed before her and she clasped her legs against his hips, keeping him buried inside her while she came so hard she was sure she would pass out.

"You're draining me, sweetheart," he purred, sounding as if he wanted her to do just that. "And if you don't let go of me, I'm going to fill you with everything I have."

Her mind was in a cloud. He grabbed her legs, prying them off his body and forcing them apart. She fought him. She wanted more, wanted him deep again. Wanted to come that hard again. And again.

Josh pulled out of her pussy, leaving her clenching and fighting to keep him buried inside her.

"I'm sorry, sweetheart. But you can't have this, not yet." And he spilled his come over her abdomen.

* * * * *

Chan closed the bathroom door behind her and listened to the sound of Josh's footsteps in the hallway and then on the stairs. She glanced at the small opaque window that looked as if it opened toward her on a chain. The house was old, and although appeared solid, was filled with windows that weren't so easy to crawl out of.

What she wouldn't do for a hot shower in her own apartment. She chewed her lip and stared at the window. Although small, and at about shoulder level, she could get out of it, depending on how far it opened. She reached up, leaning into it on tiptoe, and struggled to twist the lock that secured it. When it finally turned, she saw the lack of paint underneath, which told her how long since it had been opened.

The window fell toward her but then stopped when it reached the end of the chain it was fastened to. There wasn't even a foot's space. It was a window designed for a bathroom, a natural way of dehumidifying and allowing steam out from a hot shower. She might be able to escape if she broke the chain. Unfortunately, being an honorable female, she wouldn't destroy the owls' nest, even if it was just a damned chain.

If she changed into her fur, possibly she could jump out of the window that way. She didn't know what was on the other side though. The window opened on to the side of the house and all she had a good look of when she was outside was the front. One thing she did know—there weren't any neighbors.

A shower first would at least cleanse the smell off her. Running in her fur and reeking of a male's come might offer protection, but it might also cause less honorable rogues to think she ran from a male, and therefore was prime for the taking. Stripping out of her torn clothing, she dropped them on top of her backpack and turned on the water. Steam quickly filled the room and she stepped into the most glorious shower as hot water pelted against her sore body.

She stood under the spray, enjoying the wonderful massage it offered while her mind went over all the events of the evening and then focused on the incredible sex she'd just experienced. Josh's efforts to appease her with talk of their fucking being simply a mutual physical release pissed her off. But why?

"Because he's annoying," she told herself, letting the water soak her hair and then noticing a generic bottle of shampoo and conditioner on the ledge of the tub. She remembered smelling her own lie when she commented on the sex being no more than something casual. "And you know he smelled it. Like he needs something else to gloat about."

Her sour mood increased as she used the cheap products. She should be appreciative that her hostess supplied the bathroom with toiletries and not pout over their quality. Chan loved her scented shampoo and conditioner and the expensive soap and creams she always indulged in. She'd thrown a change of clothes into her backpack but not toiletries. If it weren't for Josh, she would have them now.

Or would it be worse?

She remembered the conversation he'd had with Charles on the phone earlier. He told her littermate two males showed up just as they left her apartment. Josh worried that Leo didn't trust him to be with her.

"Why wouldn't they trust him?"

Another thought hit her that bugged her even more. Maybe it wasn't Josh's skills that were in question. Maybe this Leo Pard male also saw visions, or worked with someone who did. It never crossed her mind before that she might not be the only one seeing her future. Imagining there might be another leopard who saw the path where she would run made her feel more violated than if she'd been raped.

"I need answers." She continued scrubbing herself, using the soap provided and hating that it didn't lather or have a scent of any kind. "And I need to quit sniffing around possibilities. What matters in the future doesn't mean a damned thing if I can't live through the night."

The steam around her faded and she no longer felt the hot water pelting her skin. Suddenly she stared at an endless gray sky, her clothes hanging on her oddly and a cold breeze chilling her flesh. Anger tightened her insides and she looked around, but her view was impaired by long, thick gray obstacles. She tried focusing on them but couldn't. She sniffed the air and almost gagged on the smell of diesel fuel and leopards, lots of leopards. And they didn't smell as if they'd just enjoyed a nice hot shower. Her ability to smell was fine, but for some reason she couldn't clear her vision.

"Do you remember any of this?" a deep male voice said.

She tried lifting her hand to wipe her eyes but couldn't. She tried harder. Then she used all the muscle she could gather and fought with all her might to lift her hand.

Chan swallowed shower water and coughed, banging her hand against the ceiling when she raised it too quickly. She pressed her hand against the shower wall while she blinked droplets off her eyelashes. "What the fuck?" she whispered, still cold although the shower water was hot.

Usually her visions were of her hovering over herself, viewing a scene while not being part of it. But this time it was different. She felt cold, and the clothes. Chan looked down at her naked, wet body. What she'd just experienced was so real, so...unnerving. Her body felt weird, as if she were filthy and sore. She grabbed the bar of soap and scrubbed her flesh ruthlessly while doing her best not to think about a damned thing.

After dressing, checking the room and not finding Josh, Chan headed down the stairs quietly. Her body still tingled from incredible sex, and although she knew she had scrubbed herself more thoroughly than she usually did, she still smelled Josh all over her. Maybe that was why he'd pushed so hard to fuck her. Obviously he'd wanted to, possibly he'd fucked her so anyone else in this nest would assume she was his mate. Already she knew he didn't want anyone here to know her true identity.

Speculating on whether or not he'd seduced her with a premeditated agenda didn't improve her mood any.

The living room was so crowded with leopards no one noticed her slipping down the stairs. A hallway led into the packed room, but also opened to other rooms that were quiet and didn't have anyone in them. She walked through a dark sitting room lined with shelves that were full of books and other keepsakes. The clean smell of happiness was about as thick as the dusty smell of so many books. Another doorway on the other side of the room led into the kitchen.

Penny stood with her back to Chan wiping the counter and whistling quietly to herself. A playpen was pushed up against the wall, layered with blankets and three owlets sleeping contentedly alongside each other. Penny turned around and then straightened when she noticed Chan, her large eyes looking quickly at her babies and then at Chan.

"They're beautiful," Chan said quietly.

Penny nodded, her expression softening. "And a handful," she said in her soothing tone. "Don't breed until you're ready."

"I won't." Chan wasn't sure she would ever be ready.

"Your male is outside with a few of the others," Penny offered, moving to the refrigerator.

Chan remembered the rule about not entering the kitchen and so remained in the doorway. She almost said Josh wasn't her male, but wasn't sure she was ready for any of the questions that might follow.

Penny didn't seem disturbed by her silence but pulled out several wrapped plates and placed them on the counter. Within minutes she prepared a hefty meat sandwich and then handed it to Chan along with a plastic cup filled with cold milk.

"You may eat in the den." Penny didn't bother telling her where the den was.

Chan sipped at the milk. "This is very kind of you."

Penny was quite a bit taller than Chan and very thin. Her clothes hung on her, hiding any figure she may or may not have. But her expression was calm, content if not almost friendly. She didn't smile, but stared directly into Chan's eyes.

"Our nest is always open to any species." She turned around and after a quick glance at her owlets, started putting the plates back in the refrigerator.

"Would you like some help?"

Penny shot her a quick glance. "I don't like anyone in my kitchen." Her tone was almost cross, but then her manner softened. "But thank you."

Chan nodded then hesitated, her stomach growling at the smell of the meat on the sandwich, but her curiosity piqued. Possibly Penny could offer her some answers, but if she asked too many, she would bring suspicion on herself. Josh had introduced her as a hunter, not as a leopard brought in and swept away from her life.

"Are all of the hunters here?" she asked.

"No. Just you four." Penny finished putting the dishes away and glanced out the window over her sink. "I did hear that all but one on the list are now brought in. Sounds like good news, except for your male. I heard he might face reprimand for letting her get away."

"Who told you that?"

Penny walked toward her and Chan stepped aside so the female could leave the kitchen. "Tore told him when they were still in here."

"Tore doesn't know everything," she said quietly, and was glad when Penny didn't look surprised.

Chan followed her into the dark room she walked through to get to the kitchen and paused when Penny turned on a lamp and nodded to a couch. Chan accepted the offer, sitting, and then placed her plate on the coffee table in front of her.

"Eat," Penny ordered, and sat in an upright chair facing Chan. "I remember a few years back when there was trouble in one of the Canadian werewolf packs. Birdie and I opened our nest to them and quite a few stayed for a day or so before moving on. Those times weren't so different from now. Almost all of them were concerned that who they were, or what they were about, be kept a secret." She shook her head, relaxing into the chair and crossed her long, thin arms over her chest.

"You've run a sanctuary for all kinds for a long time now then," Chan mused, and took a large bite of her sandwich. The meat was fresh and good. It was all she could do not to tear into the food with greed. "I remember hearing about a lunewulf pack that tried passing a law saying every female got to mate with three males. Doesn't sound like such a bad deal to me," she added, smiling at the female owl.

Penny tilted her head as if listening for something, but then returned her attention to Chan. "Trust me, one male is enough to handle. I didn't blame any of those lunewulfs for running and trying to find a better pack. And I don't blame the leopards for gathering all of you together with special gifts."

Chan focused on her sandwich, savoring the tender meat. Penny seemed content to let her eat and not hurry off. Which was good. Possibly she would learn more through this owl. Odd that someone from such a different species might know more about her kind than Chan did.

"I'm sure you know that our instructions were direct without a lot of details added." She remembered the mysterious way Josh explained learning about the job of gathering everyone on the list. Penny probably knew what went on in her nest, so Chan would run with the assumption the female knew at least as much as Chan did. "You're very kind to allow so many leopards to descend on you at once. How much notice did you get that we were arriving?"

"We think of our nest as a boarding house for those who need it." Penny spoke so softly, her voice so relaxed it was hard to imagine her as being able to handle some of the species that might take advantage of her generosity. "Tore and Josh both have stayed here before and are always welcome. Tore spoke with Birdie a few days ago. That's when we found out our nest would be a perfect location for you to rest before they come for you." She tilted her head again, this time focusing intently on Chan with her large, non-blinking eyes. "Of course, our nest is never guarded, and we don't ask questions if anyone were to leave suddenly. As long as you respect my nest while you're here then you may always come back. Birdie and I never ask questions and we don't offer information to others on who stays here or when they leave."

"It sounds like you have quite a few boarders here now. I'm sure keeping track of everyone would be quite a chore." Chan noticed immediately that Penny said a perfect location for *you* to rest, and not for those being gathered to rest. She smelled the hints offered her and wondered why the owl wanted her to know she wouldn't tell if Chan ran. Obviously if Penny wanted to say more she would do it instead of dropping hints that barely smelled of anything. "If you don't have enough room, I don't have to stay here." Possibly if she pretended she took Penny's comments the wrong way she would learn more. "I can't imagine where all of us will sleep anyway."

"You want to leave before Leo arrives?" Penny looked surprised.

Chan finished off the last bite of her sandwich and then slowly drank her milk. She held the empty plate and glass in her lap and offered Penny what she prayed was a very calm-looking expression. "Leo will be pissed if he shows up and all the leopards aren't here. We still have that female to get."

"There must be something very special about that female." Penny stood and gestured for Chan to hand her the empty plate and glass. "Josh is very dedicated for a single male, not that I'm condemning your species. But Birdie speaks very highly of him. I've never heard of him not being able to finish a job."

"Who says he's finished?" Chan stood, making a move of returning her plate and cup to the kitchen herself instead of letting Penny wait on her.

Penny turned, facing Chan, and took the dish and cup from her. Several of the leopards in the other room started growling at each other and Penny lowered her head, glaring at the wall that separated the room they were in from the living room. She made a hissing sound through her teeth and then looked at Chan quickly before turning toward the kitchen.

"I'm sure your male will be successful with whatever task he is playing out," she said curtly. "Now if you'll excuse me, I need to check on my babies. If they wake up squawking, I'll put the whole lot of them out of my nest."

Chapter Six

ॐ

Josh was headed toward the house when his cell phone rang. He pulled it from his belt, picking up his pace to get away from the others. The message on his screen made him pause.

Tore came up behind him. "Who is it?"

Birdie stepped around them and reached for the door.

"I don't know." He stared at the screen—private number calling. Very few had this number, and those who did wouldn't block him and then call. He pushed the button to accept the call. "Yes," he said gruffly.

"Joshua," a deep baritone purred into his ear. "I expect you to turn Chantelle Drap over to me immediately when I arrive there."

"Who is this?" he demanded, aware of Tore and Birdie watching him.

"This is Leo Pard." There was a moment's silence as if the male expected him to comment. When Josh didn't satisfy him, the male continued. "You'll turn her over to me or die."

The line went dead.

"Problems?" Tore asked.

"Nothing I can't handle." Josh waited for Birdie to lead the way into his nest and then followed. He smelled Chan the moment he stepped into the kitchen and started walking through the dark room, following her scent.

"The male on the other end of the line sounded pretty firm. You sure there isn't something we should know about?" Tore pressed.

Josh turned around, staring the large male in the eye. "If I ever need your help, I'll ask."

"Possibly you won't know that you need help." Tore stepped into the middle of the kitchen, puffing his chest out as if his size would intimidate Josh. "I smelled your anger the moment whoever was on the other end of the line spoke. If your call has anything to do with our matter at hand here…"

"Then I'll be sure and let you know the minute you're needed," Josh snapped.

Birdie moved in between them quickly as he had several times while outside. "Penny will be pissed as hell if you wake our owlets," he said in his calm, peaceful tone.

The owl was brave as hell to jump in between two male leopards. Birdie had hometown advantage though.

Josh backed up, glancing at the stirring babies in the crib.

Penny marched into the room, moving quickly around her mate and to the owlets. "I've already been in here once to settle these three down. If you two wake them up, then you'll be sleeping in a tree tonight," she said quietly. "You should go into the living room. Your female is in there breaking up fights."

"Crap." Josh hurried out of the room and into the living room where Chan stood with her hands on her hips, glaring at a male. "What's going on here?" he asked coolly, easing up behind Chan and then pulling her back against him.

Chan twisted quickly, her body wound tight. She shot him a warning look. "Matters are under control."

"They'll be under control when you explain why I'm sitting in this room being ignored," a young male said, doing his best to turn his tone into a deep, gruff growl.

"They're under control now," Chan hissed, stabbing the young male's chest with her fingernail. "Sit down and behave before I throw you down."

"I was told I was needed for my special gift. What is this place?" a female demanded.

"Why was I dragged away from my litter, and then stuck in this room with all of these leopards?" Another female stalked toward them and grabbed Josh's arm.

Chan shoved the female backward, ripping her fingers off his biceps. "Be lucky you're not stuck in a fucking cage," she growled.

"Don't you push me, bitch. I've already had enough crap for one night." The female lunged at Chan.

Bad move. Chan grabbed the leopard's neck and shoved her back into the wall. "Don't get me started on who has had enough crap," she hissed, her words turning garbled as she spoke. "Now sit down and shut up before I render you quiet for longer than you might wish to be."

The female grabbed Chan's arm and pushed her backward, managing to get herself away from the wall before Chan physically stopped her. Josh moved in, ready to stop any fight that might break out in Birdie's nest. He needed to get Chan the hell out of there before the scene escalated into something that would have every leopard sniffing around her.

"Now this is interesting." Tore leaned in the doorway and crossed his arms, his attention on Chan.

She spun around, her long hair still damp and hanging in dark blonde ringlets. "It's going to get a hell of a lot more interesting if you don't do your job and get these leopards settled," she snapped.

The female reached for Chan and Josh stepped between them. "Sit down now," he growled.

"That's a very good idea." Birdie appeared in the other doorway. His calm, soft-spoken nature somehow stilled the room. "I apologize for not being a better host but my mate needed help with our owlets for a few minutes. For tonight, we'll have to ask a few of you to share rooms. If there's anyone you'd like to bunk with, get with them now and then follow me."

It didn't surprise Josh a bit that Birdie's announcement would turn the place into an uproar. He took advantage of the moment and grabbed Chan, ignoring her when she spun around and hissed at him. He dragged her out of the room quickly and headed to the front door. All the leopards moving at once, howling over each other, and each anxious to get in their own demands would make it harder for Tore to sniff after them and ask more questions. If Birdie threw them out, they would be in a predicament keeping the leopards contained until Leo showed up.

Although at the moment, Leo was the least of his concerns. Josh didn't respond well to threats.

"Let's go," he said, opening the front door and holding on to Chan firmly as he guided her outside.

"Where are we going?" She looked up at him as she hurried to keep up.

They walked across the yard and then into the side brush alongside the house. There wasn't anyone in the backyard anymore. Light glowed through the many windows in the large house but they quickly walked past it, into the trees and undeveloped land, and hopefully out of reach of curious eavesdroppers.

"Where are we going?" Chan repeated, tugging to release her hand from his.

Josh slowed, turning to face her and looking back toward Birdie's and the land surrounding them. "It was getting a bit crazy in there."

"No shit."

"And I'm concerned Tore will figure out who you are."

Chan searched his face, and then sighed, looking away from him while she crossed her arms. "Who are the other hunters?" she asked, focusing her attention on the tall evergreens alongside them.

"Tore Mann is here. Then there's Thad Pierce, my cousin who lives up in Minnesota. He rounded up the leopards he was asked to find and then they met up with Tore before coming here. I haven't seen him, which probably means he feels his work is done and returned home. There's also Jin Rose. I don't know much about her, but since none of the others do either, I could say that you are her."

"What do you know about her?" she asked, hugging herself when a wicked wind swept through the trees.

"Not much. And I don't think the others do either. We were rounded up via e-mail so we haven't seen each other in person," he explained. "Hunters usually work alone. I've never heard of a time when all the hunters were united to handle a matter."

She digested the information with a quick nod. "Who's the last one? You said there were five."

"His name is Race Ogden. You met him when we first arrived, but apparently he isn't here any longer. I didn't ask where he went. Hunters keep to themselves. I've got no intention of sharing my business with anyone else here, and wouldn't expect any of them to offer their agendas to me."

He ran his hand down the side of her still-damp hair and thought of pulling her into his arms. She was cold and it would get colder as it became later. A hard run would do them both some good, but if she had questions, Josh would take his time answering them. He would gain her trust faster that way, without it, they both easily could die.

"Aren't you worried about Leo showing up and hearing all of the leopards he wants aren't here?" There was a challenge in her tone.

Josh loved how her hair dried into so many little ringlets. He combed his fingers down one side of her thick strands, separating them so her hair created smooth waves, like a peaceful bay radiating the sunlight. Her scent didn't change. If she overheard something inside, or someone said something to him, she wasn't going to make it easy and simply ask about what she heard.

"Nope. Not worried at all," he offered truthfully. "Before I came inside, I received a phone call. The number was blocked but the caller said he was Leo and if I didn't turn you over to him when he arrived, I would die."

"How sweet," she snarled. "But you know, he wouldn't have called you to say that if he believed you didn't have me."

"The leopard is a coward and bully, hiding behind fucking blocked numbers." More than anything he wanted to replace her worried smell with something sweeter, like the aroma she released when she was hot as hell for him. "Regardless of what he believes, or doesn't, I'm even more determined now not to let him get his paws on you."

She shot him a furtive glance but then looked over her shoulder toward Birdie's nest. "What's going to happen to all of the leopards here?"

Josh sniffed the air, detecting something in the breeze but unable to identify it. "I'm not sure," he admitted. "This Leo male wants to create some kind of force and use all the leopards he's gathered to work for him. There are a lot of unanswered questions, and I admit, I wouldn't have agreed to any of this if my curiosity weren't piqued. If something is going on with our species, the best way to know about it is to be as close to the action as possible."

"I would agree," she said slowly. "And there's definitely something going on."

"Why do you say that?" He watched her closely, or he wouldn't have caught the quick check she did as her expression relaxed. She knew something, or saw something, and hesitated in telling him. He pulled her to him, flattening his hand over the soft curve of her ass and then cupping the side of her neck. "Chan," he said quietly. "We need to trust each other. From this point forward there won't be anyone who will watch our tails. We need to rely on each other."

"Why should I trust you?" she whispered, her tone sounding almost hurt. "I'm not even sure what it is you want from me."

He trusted his visions, otherwise he wouldn't be pushing her so hard to be with him. But it was becoming clear she didn't trust her own mind when it showed her the future. If anything, she appeared to fight it. "Who have you told that you have visions?"

She frowned, obviously thrown by the question. "No one."

"Exactly. And if I showed up and told you I knew you had visions and because of them you were coming with me, you would have attacked worse than you did."

She gave him a sly smile. "Think you couldn't have handled it?"

"I can handle you." He tightened his grip on her, tangling his fingers in her hair when she tried pushing away. "And I'll admit, I don't mind doing it."

She tilted her head, giving him an odd, almost amused look. "Do you really think you're the one doing the handling? My dear male, those leopards in there would have torn that nest up if I didn't stop them. And as for you and me," she added, looking away from him so the shadows clouded her expression. "There is no you and me."

Chan was a proud, aggressive, dominating single female. He watched her face and saw only annoyance, which meant she smelled her lie too.

"Lying isn't one of your stronger qualities," he told her quietly.

"It doesn't matter." She pushed harder until he let her go and then walked around him. "Too much shit is going on and I'm not going to confuse it with a relationship." She looked over her shoulder, her gaze softening when she stared up at him. "I'm sorry, Josh. But that's simply how it is."

If she thought he would let her walk deeper into the trees alone, she was going to learn otherwise. "How it is, little cat," he informed her, easily falling into stride next to her, "is that while this shit is going on, you're going to stay by my side. If I have to put a leash on you, so be it. But I'll be damned if I'm going to turn you over to some unknown male simply because he demands it."

"I think I'm going for a run. Burn off some energy." Her words faded as she spoke.

Josh looked down at her but didn't see her face. Instead a bright light appeared before him. He squinted, his pupils adjusted to the night and not ready for the sudden glare.

"Do you smell that?" The whispered words sounded a lot like Chan.

Josh fought not to shake his head, or squint further to bring the image in better. He wasn't seeing or hearing anything in front of him. It was in his head. Chan stood in front of him and she didn't just ask him about a particular scent. Instead, he tried relaxing his face, his mind, allowing the image to play out and tell him more.

Something moved in front of him. A person approached—not a leopard. Josh raised his gaze, looking straight ahead of him instead of down at Chan. He stared into yellow eyes. And then he was blinded.

"What?" Chan asked, touching his arm.

Josh fought to quickly adjust his eyes to the darkness. "Nothing. I...nothing."

"Nothing, huh." She turned and slid her jeans down her legs.

Josh realized she was almost naked, her long hair shrouding the upper half of her body while her firm, round ass was within hand's reach. His palms itched, but grabbing a hold of her as he ached to do would allow her to get away. Unless he wanted to tear his clothes to shreds, changing quickly without undressing, he needed to get the hell out of his clothes or she would leave without him.

"We'll run for a little bit," he told her, changing the subject and deciding he'd ponder why he just saw an image of a coyote later. "I want your word on a couple of things before we leave though."

"Oh really? You have a vision and don't tell me what it is, but then demand I give you promises." She twisted her shirt and jeans together, creating a rope out of them. "And you demand that I trust you, imply there's something between us, yet you don't trust me. I'm not promising you shit."

"Yes, you are." He yanked off his shirt but then grabbed her arm, forcing her to turn and face him. Her full, round breasts looked damned good with her hair falling down around them. And her nipples puckered in the cold, making his mouth water. It took some effort to force his gaze to her eyes. "We stay together. No exceptions. I want your word that you will not try to run off."

"Think you can't catch me?" she challenged, her pouty lips curving up into an alluring smile.

"I know that I can," he said quietly. And he knew she knew it too. "You can't outrun me as a human let alone as a leopard. I also know I can overpower you, and in our fur, if you challenge me, you'll get more than you want right now."

Her eyes were wide for only a moment before they narrowed into suspicious slits. She shivered in the cold and he let go of her arm, quickly disrobing so they could change and warm up.

"Fine. We stay together. But you give me your word too. Let's see if it's worth anything. While we're in our fur, you'll promise not to fuck me against my will."

Little bitch. God, she was good. He liked that about her more than he thought he would in a female. Not that he'd ever taken time to create a list of traits or faults he wanted or didn't want in a mate. Taking a mate never crossed his mind. And he wasn't considering it now either. But damn, she got him there. Chan knew as well as he did that in their fur, primal instinct prevailed over rational thought. He'd already fucked her once. It would be hard as hell not to take her in their fur.

"You have my word," he said.

She tilted her head, trying to see his face when he didn't look at her. "I do?" she asked, sounding surprised.

"Yes." He gripped his clothes, twisting them quickly, and then tied them around his waist. Then grabbing hers out of her hands with a bit more aggression than he needed, he reached around her naked body and then secured them at her waist. He looked down when she arched into him, letting her head fall back so she could see him easily with their bodies almost touching. He stared into her deep, milky green eyes. "You have my word, Chan. I won't fuck you unless you want me to."

She stared at him for a long moment and he didn't look away. Something changed in her expression. His words affected her, but he wasn't sure how. Instead of responding, she released the change inside her while he watched. Her eyes started glowing while suddenly tiny flecks of gold lightened the color of her eyes. Black marks, creating patterns over her body, made her even more beautiful.

"I don't want you to," she whispered, her voice huskier than usual and her words slurred like a drunk as her mouth took on new form.

She grinned, looking as though she would enjoy the hell out of torturing him now that she had his word. Josh growled, allowing the change to consume him too. But he couldn't take his eyes off her as her body curved, her creamy flesh taking on new color. Her rosettes were perfectly symmetrical, the small black circles spreading over her naked body, growing darker and more distinct as he watched. She raised her eyes to his, her smug grin looking triumphant while her eyes flashed a golden-green shade and defiance added to their glow. They altered in shape, becoming rounder while suddenly it looked as if she wore black eyeliner.

Her body swayed as though she performed some erotic dance for him, teasing and taunting while stretching before him naked.

Josh couldn't stop the aroused growl that ripped out of him. The change accelerated, altering his vision and senses. He fell to the ground, leaping and landing on top of her. Her scent violated his senses with a rich, powerful aroma. Nothing had ever smelled better.

Chan hissed ferociously, raising her hand, which turned into a paw with deadly claws as she bared her long teeth and screamed her protest. She was half his size, which worked to her advantage only because she was able to slide out from underneath him, roll over and race away.

Josh clawed at the earth, inhaling the ripe scent of fresh dirt as he leapt into the air and took off after Chan. The wind hit his face, invigorating him and feeding his drive and urge to capture her again. She was his female. Nothing would stop him, and no one would dispute him. The world was good and strong and in his favor. She could run, tear across the broken, uneven ground, dart around foliage and trees, but she wouldn't escape. That confidence fed him with intense satisfaction.

Which possibly was why it took a few minutes longer than normal for the rational side of his brain to kick in. He'd made her a promise, given his word. Josh wouldn't fuck Chan. When the knowledge seeped around the strong instincts that led his actions, he almost stumbled.

Damn her again. She was a smart little bitch. If he allowed his instinct to rule him, he would tackle her, mount her and slide inside that hot little pussy of hers. He would fuck her ruthlessly and with the savage desire that burned him alive. He would claim her and demand her complete submission. If she didn't offer it, he would overpower her, conquer her until she did.

Life was simple in his fur. Rules and accepted politeness that applied to humans didn't exist then. But his human half still thrived in his brain. Granted, rational thinking wasn't usually as strong as carnal instinct, but it still existed. And he remembered clearly the promise he just made her.

Fucking bullshit.

Josh ran, easily pacing her, letting her keep the lead. One, he could watch her easily—and damn, it was one hell of a view. And two, he protected her, not once letting his defense down as he continually glanced around them, keeping an eye out for anyone else who might be around, and then returning his attention to her sweet ass.

The fever in his brain cooled as he ran. The evergreens offered a sweet perfume that scented the cold night air. They were too far from the ocean to smell the saltiness of it, but the rough wilderness around them offered fresh, revitalizing aromas.

Running hard always cleared his brain. And it did so now. He would give Chan this, making him promise not to fuck her helped screw his brain back on properly. In his almost thirty years, Josh never once regretted his status of single male. He never dwelt on what type of female he wanted to share his life with. Having cubs or creating a solitary home weren't things he gave much thought to.

And he didn't now. Chan appealed to him. Hell yeah, it was physical. But it was more than that too. Josh wasn't bull-headed and so full of himself like so many single males that he didn't see the obvious when it came to him. No other female in his past did to him what Chan did. And that knowledge made all of this worth exploring. She wouldn't get away from him no matter what adventure lay ahead of them. Some powerful shit was about to go down. That was more than intuition speaking. At least part of it, if not all, was going to be bad. But no one ruled him. He didn't take any order he didn't want. Josh controlled his own destiny. And for now, until he explored this to his satisfaction, Chan was staying by his side. He wasn't going to let her go. At least not for now.

Chan slowed after a good hour of hard running and walked lazily alongside a good-sized stream. When she stopped and then lowered her head to take a long drink, Josh surveyed the land around them. There was wildlife and doing a bit of hunting sounded good. He looked up at the low-hanging gray clouds that cluttered the otherwise black sky. The moon was half full, bright and glowing when it appeared briefly between clouds. There was at least half the night left. Plenty of time to find a late-night snack.

When she drank her fill, Chan stretched out along the bank, her beautiful coat and elegant appearance distracting him again. Josh forced himself to look away. It was important to obtain her complete trust, and if that meant battling the strongest of his instincts, he would damned well do it.

He took his time drinking the cold, fresh water. When he straightened, Chan watched him intently with glowing gold-green eyes. She held her head high like a regal princess with her sensual body stretched out in a provocative pose. Her legs were parted enough that her scent reached him easily.

He watched her carefully. If she meant to tease him, test his limits and try to push him, he would tan her adorable tight ass. Chan purred, the rumbling sound erotic, and rolled around on the grass. She stretched her body, arching her back and spreading her legs while she rubbed her body over the rough ground.

She might wish to push him and see how long he would keep his word, but that didn't mean he needed to stand here and take it. Josh leapt over her, gaining a bit of warped satisfaction when she howled in surprise, and ran along the length of the stream. He put enough distance between them that he cleared his nose of her strong, aroused scent and breathed in fresh air. Chan could take off in the other direction and he would easily be able to catch up with her. He turned his back on her, taking a deep breath and watching the wilderness around them.

Other than a few rabbits, he didn't smell any larger wildlife. Not that he was surprised. They weren't exactly quiet while racing across the open land.

Chan leapt at him from behind. Her smaller body crashed into his and he turned, instinct dominating, and flipped her off him. Then jumping, he clamped down on the loose fur at the back of her neck and dragged her to him, keeping her from tumbling into the water.

Josh let go of her and she tumbled to the side, shaking her head fiercely and then looking up at him. He glanced at her but didn't have time to register on whether he'd pissed her off or turned her on more. Behind Chan stood another leopard.

"Head on back now. It's time to call it a night." It was his mother's voice.

Josh blinked, every inch of him hardening while a chill rushed over him with a fierceness that matched a hard winter wind. He didn't realize Chan growled at him until she leaped toward his face. Josh barely had time to jump out of her way before getting mauled by the fiery little bitch.

He regained his composure quickly and looked around them. Turning in a half circle, he breathed in sharply and smelled nothing other than Chan and the wilderness around them. The other leopard was gone.

Chapter Seven

๛

Chan entered the owls' nest just before dawn, adjusting her shirt and then combing her tangled hair with her fingers. They weren't the only ones awake.

"Where have you been?" Tore came down the stairs, barely making a sound for a leopard of his size. He wasn't taller than Josh, but he was buffed out like one of those wrestlers on TV.

Definitely too muscular for Chan's tastes.

"We went for a run." Josh wasn't acting right, and hadn't since they changed back into their skin.

If he was pissed at her for pushing him, then he would just have to get over it. She had a right to know if she could trust him to keep to his word or not. And as turned-on as it made her, she was proud of him for not breaking. Granted, now she was horny as hell, but it felt good knowing her opinion of him wasn't misguided. He didn't smell like a liar and he'd kept his word not to fuck her in his fur. Of course now they weren't in their fur anymore.

"What's going on here?" Josh asked Tore.

"Jin Rose is here," Tore offered, and then looked at Chan. "I'm guessing that means you are our missing Chantelle Drap."

She hated the triumphant smile he gave Josh.

"She's none of your business," Josh growled.

"If she's on the list, she sure as hell is," Tore said quickly. "Leo called me while you were out with your female. He's very anxious to meet our hot little Chantelle." His smile turned provocative when he let his gaze travel down her. "There must be something incredibly appealing about you."

"You really don't want to find out," she snarled, and then headed around him toward the stairs.

Josh followed her into their room but then hesitated at the door. There was only one bed and they hadn't discussed sleeping arrangements. When she turned and saw his perplexed expression, she wondered if something else wasn't bothering him.

"I'm going back downstairs," he said without looking at her. Already he had turned and put his hand on the doorknob. "Lock the door when I leave and don't let anyone in but me."

"Okay…" she said, drawing the word out. She walked toward him slowly, but he left the room, closing the door silently behind him. "You're one interesting leopard," she whispered, and twisted the lock on the doorknob.

If she wasn't so damned exhausted, she would follow him and check out the other hunters. But sleep sounded way too good and at least this way, if Josh wanted to crash later, she could give him the bed and do her investigating after a few hours of shut-eye. And without Josh trailing her.

She was stiff as hell when she woke up and very much alone. No one bothered her while she showered, although by the many voices and overlapping smells, it was obvious there were a lot of leopards in the nest. She excused herself past several others waiting to use the bathroom, and headed down the hall.

"Do you buy into all they're telling us?" A female about her age stopped her and put her cool fingers on Chan's arm.

Normally Chan didn't care for strangers touching her. She stared into the pale green eyes of the female and didn't smell any aggressiveness on her.

"I'm not sure what to think," she answered, knowing her response wouldn't smell like a lie since she honestly didn't know. She was clueless as to what the female was talking about. "What do you think of all of it?"

"Well, they say we're all gifted, and if attending their class can bring something special out of me, I guess I'm game. Have you ever noticed anything odd about you?" The female sniffed as she asked and brushed her fingers over her curly red hair. She wore a ring on every damned finger.

"Not really." Again not a lie. Chan didn't think her visions were odd, they were just part of her. "What would they teach us in a class though?"

The female studied Chan's face for a moment, and Chan didn't blame her for being cautious. All of this was so bizarre, and her guess was the rest of them remained here out of morbid curiosity.

"I got to talk to Jin, the female?" she said, lowering her voice and glancing down the hall at the leopards who chatted among themselves in hushed whispers while waiting for the bathroom. "She didn't seem too interested in talking to me, but she did give me a minute and answered at least one of my questions."

"What question was that?" Chan matched her hushed tone.

"I asked her how long we would be here."

"And?"

"She said they're putting everyone through a series of tests in this class, and those who don't meet the levels of psychic behavior they want to see will be allowed to go home."

"Just like that?"

The young female frowned and puckered her lips. She was cute but smelled almost too gullible. "Just like that," she said finally, and then looked up at Chan quickly, as if anticipating some kind of reaction.

Chan smiled, keeping her expression and her thoughts relaxed. "Cool," she said, and then patted the young female's arm. "Good luck."

"Yeah."

Chan looked down the hallway. A female, possibly in her thirties, reached the top of the stairs and stared at her, her piercing green eyes all-knowing and her scent rich with human perfume. Her dyed black hair, eyeliner and black clothing added to her mystique. Chan blinked, the vision fading just as the female who had been talking to her opened her mouth to speak.

"I guess I'll talk to you later," the young female in front of her said. "I'm going to catch a nap."

"See you." Chan looked at the stairs as the sound of shoes tapped against the wooden steps. The woman she just saw in her mind reached the top of the stairs and met her gaze. Again Chan smelled the rich perfume. But there was something else in the air, something that screamed at Chan to be careful.

"You don't look much like me." The female spoke softly, not condemning, but definitely with her guard up.

"You're right." Chan studied green eyes that were so bright she wondered if the female wore contacts.

"If you're going to pretend to be me at least you should have tried playing the part."

Chan didn't see any reason to respond and thought about turning and leaving the female, whom she guessed to be Jin Rose, standing alone in the hallway.

"You weren't at the meeting this morning." Her voice was soft, husky, her green eyes intense.

"I didn't get an invitation." Instantly Chan raised all shields. Something about this female demanded caution. Chan relaxed her mind, her thoughts, her body, doing her damnedest to keep her scent neutral and calm.

"It was posted downstairs."

"I haven't been downstairs." Chan picked up the strong smell of leather as she moved to walk past the female.

"I'm Jin Rose," the female told her, turning to prevent Chan from passing her. Jin's black leather pants made a gentle sifting sound when she moved. "And you are?"

"Chantelle Drap," she said without hesitating, although she was certain Jin already knew this. In spite of Jin's efforts to hide her scent with human smells, Chan sensed the female was strong, and Chan wouldn't hide behind ambiguity and appear weak. "Was there something you wanted?"

When Jin smiled, she looked younger. And for a moment Chan picked up on hesitation. She was trying to appear confident, but something inside Chan told her Jin wasn't any more sure of herself than Chan was. They were equals.

"Yes actually, you." Jin glanced up and down the hallway. "I just got here and the nest is very full. But I'd like to talk to you."

Chan didn't see any reason why she shouldn't take Jin into her room. It wasn't as if the female could overpower her. And Chan's curiosity was piqued, although she didn't doubt for a moment Jin wanted her feeling just that way.

Jin followed her to the room, neither of them speaking. Chan let Jin enter first and then closed the door, turning the lock on the doorknob behind her while she watched Jin check out the simple quarters.

"You slept alone," Jin mused.

"I usually do," Chan said, walking slowly into the room and taking her time checking out Jin further while the female had her back to her.

Jin would probably be what most males considered a knockout, tail worth chasing and fighting for. Her style of dress would make her stand out, and more than likely create a fight if she entered a room with single males. Chan guessed Jin was probably the kind of female who enjoyed that kind of attention.

"Who do you sleep with?" she asked, deciding the questioning wouldn't be one-sided.

Jin turned around to face her, again smiling. "No one," she said. "But I don't want to compare our sexual experiences. You probably know Leo is very interested in you."

"If he even exists."

"He does." Jin's expression grew serious. "He'll be here tonight."

"So you've met him?" Chan crossed her arms over her chest. In the small room with no other leopards around all of Jin's human smells she used didn't prevent her own scent from seeping through. Chan smelled caution, possibly fear. She decided to push a bit and learn how strong this female actually was.

"How well do you know him?" Chan guessed this female believed she possessed abilities strong enough to merit attention. Keeping her emotions under lock and key and focusing on her heartbeat, on keeping it slow and relaxed, she walked closer to Jin, clasping her hands behind her and started a slow circle around the female. "Are his strengths as apparent as his weaknesses?"

Chan smelled surprise.

"There's nothing weak about Leo," Jin said almost reverently. "And yes, I've met him. That's why I'm here. He wants you, Chantelle, very badly."

"Obsession is another weakness."

"He's not obsessed. He's determined and he's very, very smart." Jin sounded as if she really wanted Chan to believe this. There was something about her imploring tone that flagged questions in Chan. "He sees in leopards what no one else saw."

"That we can be exploited?" Chan demanded, speaking before giving it much thought. Her question gained a rise out of Jin though, which was very interesting. "Does he really think that if someone really possessed abilities others didn't have that they would willingly turn their freedom over to some coward who hides behind an urban myth?"

Whatever emotion Chan inhaled from Jin, it faded quickly. Jin walked over to the window, releasing the smell of leather and her musky perfume in the air. She dragged her fingers through her straight black hair and stared outside.

"I didn't seek you out to sell Leo to you. What you think of him really doesn't matter to me."

"Why did you seek me out then?"

Jin turned around, her lips thin with determination. "To tell you to run," she whispered. "Get the hell out of here. Don't tell anyone where you're going and disappear."

* * * * *

Chan wondered for the hundredth time if she were doing the right thing. Although Jin told her to run and head north where the snow and frozen ground and mountains would make it harder to track her, Chan decided to take Jin's initial instructions to heart. No one would know which direction she went.

She stared out the window of the large bus, growing more and more nauseous from the smell of human sweat. Five hours of sitting in the uncomfortable seat, feeling claustrophobic and surrounded by humans, and she only had thirty-four more hours to go before reaching Phoenix.

She would never make it.

"I've got to pee," she told the human driver when they pulled into a convenience store in St. George, Utah.

Humans slept in most of the seats, and the weary-looking driver grunted, marking something on a clipboard and not bothering to look at her. "We leave in ten minutes whether you're on the bus or not."

"I'll be back." She hurried off, gulping in the fresh air as she ran across the parking lot to the convenient store.

Half an hour later, she paid for her candy bar and strolled across the lot, ignoring the store clerk's concern that she'd missed her bus. As she crossed the street, anxious to leave the town and all the smells that prevented her from breathing in nature, her cell phone buzzed and then started chirping.

"Who is this?" Her stomach turned into anxious knots as she recognized the Phoenix area code. "Charles has my cell phone number?"

Josh would have had to give it to him, but how would he have learned it? She pushed the button to answer the call, refusing to let her thoughts go in the direction of Josh. She'd met him the day before yesterday, and she was level-headed enough not to fall for some male when she barely knew him.

"Hello," she said, keeping a quick pace and hurrying down the street.

"Where in the hell are you?" It wasn't Charles. Josh sounded mad as hell.

"How did you get my number?" Chan almost stumbled over her feet as her tummy did a number that almost sent the candy bar back up her throat.

"The same way I found you. I'm good." His deep baritone rushed over her, making her face flush and her skin tingle.

It was wrong to be turned-on simply by hearing his voice. "You better be really good. If you let anyone know you're talking to me..."

"I'm not a fucking idiot, except that I trusted you and you ran," he growled. "Tell me where you are and I'll meet you. And why did you leave me?"

He didn't sound hurt, did he?

"Well, I won't say a little birdie told me." She kept her pace, anxious to leave the town behind her. Heading north, she could find shelter in the canyons until she figured out what exactly was going on. "Did Leo Pard show up?"

"Actually, no. Someone tipped him off that you weren't here. He's delayed his arrival and ordered a search for you. You sure as hell better not be anywhere obvious."

"That's very interesting. And don't worry. They won't find me." Now that she knew she was being hunted, she would be damn sure to stay out of sight. The question was, for how long?

"Tell me where you are."

She picked up her pace, seeing the last of the homes ahead of her before open space lined either side of the road.

"Chan," he said quietly, his voice sounding so good in her ear. "Last night you demanded I not touch you in my fur. I gave you my word and kept it. Do you know how fucking hard that was to do, especially with you tempting the shit out of me?"

"I'm sorry." She grinned, her insides warming when she thought of him struggling to not fuck her. "I know I told you you didn't have honor. You do, Josh. Thank you."

"Good. I'm glad we've established that fact," he grumbled. "Now tell me where the fuck you are."

It would be a hell of a lot nicer staying out of sight and not being alone. She sighed and admitted to herself reluctantly that she wanted to see him again. "I tell you what, call me in the morning. Once you're sure you aren't being followed then I'll meet you."

She hung up her cell phone and then quickly turned it off. Suddenly the darkness around her seemed a hell of a lot colder and the open space was a lot more open. Being alone didn't usually bother her, but Josh's concerned tone, his demands that he be with her created an ache that grew the longer she walked. The best thing to do was get off the road, change into her fur and then find a quiet spot somewhere in the Snow Canyon State Park. The emptiness inside her grew, wrapping around her heart and making it hurt like hell. It was going to be one long night.

When she opened her eyes and stretched over the flat rock she'd found the night before to sleep on, it dawned on her that being in her fur, waking up to a glorious sunrise, was something she'd dreamed of doing. She didn't need to hurry out the door to work among humans. There was no concern about bills, or if her hair lay right, or how her makeup looked. None of the stress of being in her flesh existed at the moment.

Chan rolled onto her back, rubbing against the flat rock and purring at the pleasure of her self-inflicted back rub. She blinked, staring upside down at the canyon that stretched out around her. Wildlife surrounded her. She could smell breakfast and the thought of chasing down and killing fresh meat should make her invigorated.

The emptiness gnawing at her insides wasn't from hunger though.

Damn him, she rumbled. *He's not going to crawl under my skin like this.* Josh might be an incredible male, but that didn't mean he was right for her. *He showed up in my life to steal me away all because of some urban myth.* And he gave her his word not to touch her in his fur, and kept it. Chan might not be male, but she knew in his fur instinct would have ruled. It took a hell of a lot of willpower on his part to keep his promise to her.

Why did he do it?

She sprawled lazily on the large rock and crossed her paws over each other, gazing down at the black rocks below. Birds flew overhead, large hawks and smaller, faster-moving sparrows. The sky was turning into incredible shades of pinks and pale blues as the sun slowly woke up on the horizon. It would be good hunting this morning.

Chan didn't move though. Her clothes were still twisted around her waist and would be wrinkled as hell. That didn't bother her either. She needed to pull them off her, stash them safely with her backpack and boots and prowl the canyon until she found herself a feast. Instead, memories of fucking Josh, of feeling him buried deep, filled the emptiness inside her with a growing pressure that ate at her miserably. What would it be like to fuck him in her fur?

Just imagining his powerful body next to hers, his coarse hair tickling and teasing while he nipped and clawed her flesh, had her panting. She stretched out on her belly, feeling her pussy swell and fill the air around her with a rich, musky scent. Fucking Josh in her fur would be nothing like in their flesh. He was almost twice her size.

That thought almost made her come.

God. Quit this. Chan jumped to her feet, suddenly grouchy and hating that she was miserable too. *He's not here and he's not going to be here. So just get over it.* Shifting her weight was enough to make the pressure inside her throb into an impossible craving. Her body swelled, her pussy preparing itself to be fucked. When she walked the length of the flat rock that was her bed the night before, moisture soaked her fur between her hind legs. Thoughts of him climbing over her from behind, wrapping his front paws around her so she couldn't move and impaling her with his thick, swollen cock almost made her stagger.

His weight would be too much for her. No matter how hard she tried to stand, she would topple over. Josh would keep her pinned, lowering his hind end until his large cock pressed against her soaked pussy.

I should have let him fuck me when we went on that run. At least then she would have the memory. Not that her imagination wasn't doing a damn good job of making her just as hot as remembering if they actually had fucked. She saw it in her head as if it really happened. This wasn't a vision that toyed with her mind. There wasn't the realness to it, just her overactive imagination wishing and dreaming about what possibly would never happen.

And why? Because some female she didn't even know encouraged her to run.

No. She wouldn't confuse the issues. Craving Josh had nothing to do with leopards wanting her because she saw things others didn't. Maybe Leo Pard was responsible for her meeting Josh, but what happened now — today and tomorrow — wouldn't be motivated by his actions. If Josh reentered her life, it would be because she willed it.

And I can't let him into my life just because I can't wait to fuck him again. Although at the moment, that sounded like a damn good reason. Chan wasn't stupid though. There were other qualities Josh possessed besides being an incredible piece of tail. He'd kept his word when he was in his fur. That went a long way. It showed her he was strong and capable of agreeing to something and then carrying it out.

Which was probably why the urban myth sought him out as a hunter. She wasn't the only one who saw the good in Josh.

Chan sat and used her mouth to remove her clothes. Her cell phone fell free from her jeans. Josh would call her soon if he learned he wasn't being followed. She wasn't able to push the buttons with her paws, but gently touching it with one claw caused it to light up. There were no missed calls.

They're going to follow him. You know they are.

God damn it. She would be miserably depressed before the sun was above the horizon. Putting her clothes in her backpack and pushing it against the back of the rock, she then tucked her cell phone in the side pocket of her bag. Her wallet with all of her credit cards was still in her jeans. Her things were safe for now. She turned and leapt down the rocks. It was time to find breakfast and then decide what she would do with the rest of her day.

When she reached the grassy valley, a new scent grabbed her attention. Chan sleeked along the ground, searching around her and breathing in the disturbing smell. Then she spotted several objects running across the open area ahead of her.

Crap. Coyotes.

There were four of them, but oftentimes with coyotes, where there were several, more lay in hiding, waiting. Chan had never met a coyote, but from what she'd heard, they weren't to be trusted. She wouldn't judge anyone without knowing them, but nonetheless, she kept low and moved back toward the rocks.

Coyotes were small, usually didn't get along with humans and kept to themselves in packs like the werewolves. She searched her memory for any remnants of knowledge she might have heard in her past about them. When she came up blank, she kicked herself for not thinking it through that the Snow Canyon State Park would be an ideal home for them.

Loud barking overhead startled the crap out of her. Chan looked up quickly and her heart exploded in her chest. Several coyotes leered down at her. She raced out of the way when one of them jumped down toward her.

Get the fuck away from me, she howled, and then bulldozed into the creep who thought he could take her down. Blood filled her mouth when she tore into his flesh. But there were too many of them. Chan swung out with extended claws, bit and lunged, but they kept coming at her. Suddenly they were all on top of her, howling and barking furiously. All she saw were large white fangs and drooling, despicable grins.

They all disappeared as her world of brown fur faded away. This wasn't a good time for a vision to hit her. She growled furiously as a bright light blinded her and she raised her hands to cover her eyes.

"That's her. Good job. We'll take her from here." It was the same voice she'd heard before in her other vision.

The image disappeared and her world went black.

Chapter Eight

ɛ૭

Josh threw his cell down on the bed, growling in irritation. Why the fuck wasn't she answering her phone? Someone rapped on his hotel room door and he looked up, his eyes narrowing as he sniffed and tried to figure out who was out there without saying anything. The maids wouldn't be bothering him in the middle of the afternoon, and he hadn't called room service. Moving silently to the door, he remained calm as the knock sounded again.

"Josh, it's Birdie. Let me in."

He hadn't thought it a problem letting the owl know where he'd be crashing when he left the nest the night before. Nonetheless, trepidation tightened his gut at the sound of the owl's calm, soothing tone.

Josh pulled open the door and frowned. "What in the hell are you doing here?" he asked, surprised and glancing both ways down the disinfected hallway.

"Penny's holding down the nest." The tall, thin male suddenly sounded stressed.

"What's wrong?" Josh stepped to the side, letting the owl inside the hotel room.

"We just got word from some owls we know in Utah, around St. George. There is a coyote pack there and one of the owls spotted them taking out a leopard. That doesn't usually happen. Coyotes don't attack unless there's profit in it, or they're starving." Birdie ran his long fingers through his gray hair. His hair was pulled into a small ponytail at his neck and a few strands were loose. He tried tucking them behind his ear, scowling at the floor. "They aren't starving and something isn't right."

Josh glanced at his cell phone, knowing Chan would see his missed calls. She wasn't calling him back yet.

"I contacted the bus system. She bought a one-way ticket to Phoenix. I talked to her last night and she wouldn't tell me where she was, but according to their schedule, she'll arrive in Phoenix tonight."

Birdie's gray eyes didn't blink when he stared at Josh. "She might have gotten on that bus, but she got off in Utah, not Arizona. The nest who contacted me are good birds. We stay out of others' problems, but we don't stand by and do nothing when there's something wrong. Your female is with those coyotes. Go get her."

Josh stared at Birdie as he turned to the door. "How are you so sure?" he asked, his stomach twisting at the thought of Chan in the hands of coyotes.

"Make sure you get her before the others do," Birdie said, and then opened the hotel room door and left, closing it quietly behind him.

"Crap." Josh snatched up his phone, punching the redial number with his finger and then growled when it rang until going to voice mail. "God damn it. Why did I let her get away?"

Grabbing his jacket and stuffing his wallet and change in his back pocket, Josh stormed out the door, leaving the room key on the bed. By midafternoon he pulled into a convenience store in St. George, Utah. He needed to fill his tank and then get a feel for the place.

"Are you here for a reason, leopard?"

Josh stood alongside his car, reaching for the gas pump, and turned around to stare into shrewd-looking pale yellow-green eyes.

"Do you want to pump the gas for me?" he demanded, keeping his voice low and searching the coyote's face.

"No. I want to know why you're here." The coyote male didn't glance around them but stood with confidence, his expression and tone relaxed as if they were doing no more than discussing the weather.

Josh knew a few things about coyotes, most being that they were a very misunderstood race. Their reputation for being heartless and money hungry wasn't completely inaccurate. But they were loyal as hell to their own. And if a coyote viewed someone as a friend, he had their back until death.

"I was sent here," he told the coyote honestly. "There's a possibility a female leopard was injured near this area."

"Get your gas. I'll wait for you." The coyote left him, walking with a lazy stroll across the parking lot to a running SUV parked in a stall in front of the convenience store.

Josh filled his tank and paid for the gas. The coyote pulled out of his stall as soon as Josh was behind his driver's wheel. A few minutes later, Josh followed the SUV around the backside of a warehouse where there were several loading docks. The coyote parked alongside one, got out of his car and walked up to Josh.

"Stay here," he instructed. "Stay in your car. No one will bother you."

"Where are you going?" Josh didn't like the tingles from nerves that crawled over his skin. He squinted up at the coyote, who was busy looking around the empty parking lot and at the loading docks. "Why did you bring me here?"

"Because our females aren't too keen on other species entering their dens," he said smoothly, giving Josh a placid look. His expression turned shrewd in the next moment. "I'll be back soon. Stay here."

The coyote returned to his SUV and drove off, leaving Josh to chill out behind a warehouse building with empty docks. He shut off his car and climbed out, glancing around the lot and then up at the opened garage doors that looked like hallowed eyes staring blindly at him. The place was thick with the smell of coyotes. Obviously St. George was home to a good-sized pack.

Did Chan get off the bus here? He noticed the gas station was also a bus stop. If he hadn't been so distracted by the coyote, he would have thought to ask the clerks if they'd seen Chan. But then maybe that was why the coyote was there, to distract anyone who might come around asking questions.

But what interest would coyotes have in a leopard female?

Ten minutes seemed more like several hours. Josh leaned against the door to his car, arms crossed, and scowled while he tried figuring out why the coyote would want him to wait here when another car pulled around the side of the building. The well-built male driving wore sunglasses, but when he parked and got out, standing maybe five foot eight at the most, Josh guessed him to be another coyote. A car pulled in behind him and the male walked over to the driver. Whatever words were exchanged, it didn't please whoever was in the second car. The first car left and Josh found himself staring at the driver who more than likely was instructed to wait just as he was.

What the hell was going on here?

A tall, older male got out of the newer, rather expensive-looking sports car and approached him slowly. Josh noticed immediately he was a leopard and that he wasn't alone. There was someone else waiting in the car.

"You may leave now. Your services are no longer needed." The male's voice sounded strangely familiar. "Your name has been removed from the list."

"And you are?" Josh squinted at the male.

"You were hired as a hunter, the terms being you would be compensated for your time and trouble once your task was completed." The male stood about the same height as Josh but was thicker, more mature, but definitely not in his prime. He reached for his back pocket, the thick, pungent smell of leather filling the air when the leather jacket he wore made crinkling sounds as he moved. "Your services are no longer needed," he repeated, and pulled out a wallet, opened it, revealing a thick stack of bills. "What you've done is greatly appreciated though, and the terms are being honored now." He pulled out most of the bills. "Here's three thousand dollars, which should more than cover your expenses."

"I don't know," Josh said, taking the bills and stuffing them in his back pocket. "The cost of gas is outrageous these days."

The male's expression remained blank as he stared at Josh. If the male wanted to size him up, he could go ahead and do so. If he wanted Josh to take the cash and run, he wasn't going to get his wish.

"That it is," the male said slowly. "How much more do you need?"

"It depends on what you're paying me for." Josh realized where he heard the voice before, the threatening phone call before demanding that he turn Chan over the following day. "If you're paying me for Chantelle, I'm afraid I don't have her."

The male grinned, showing off bright, large white teeth. "I know you don't. I have her."

Josh didn't need a second to think about his next action. Hauling back, he took his fist and felt incredible satisfaction when he pounded the large male's face. Blood splattered as the male staggered backward. His large teeth didn't look quite so white anymore as he sneered at Josh.

"You will never have her," Josh growled, lunging toward the male.

Surprisingly, the male jumped out of Josh's path. He touched his fingers to his nose as blood spewed over his mouth and chin. Its metallic smell drowned out the smell of anger that would otherwise probably dominate. The male glared at Josh, keeping part of his face covered as he stuffed his wallet back in his pants. Then surprisingly, he continued backing away from Josh as he pulled out a cotton handkerchief and used it to blot his nose.

"Consider yourself paid," he said with a nasally tone. The male looked at the end of the building quickly.

Josh glanced that direction too, assuming someone else had arrived. There wasn't a car there. It was just the two of them and the passenger who remained sitting in the male's car. He looked back at the male, who kept the handkerchief over his nose and frowned at the spot where a car would appear when it drove around the building.

Josh looked back quickly when a car drove into the parking area and pulled up in front of them. The coyote who brought him here sat in the driver's seat of a different vehicle. Josh scowled when the injured male hurried to the car. It was as if he knew the car was coming. Very interesting.

The coyote jumped out. "What happened to you?"

"Don't worry about it. Is she here?" The male waved his hand in the air, the other still covering his face and making his voice sound not only nasally but muffled.

"Yup." The coyote shifted his attention to Josh only for a moment. He then moved to the rear of the car and popped open the trunk.

Josh hurried along to the opposite side of the other two and looked in the back of the car at the same time the stranger and the coyote did.

"That's her. Good job. We'll take her from here." The male gestured with his free hand to the person in the car.

"You aren't taking her anywhere," Josh hissed, pushing the coyote out of the way and reaching into the back of the car. "Chan, can you hear me? Chan."

Chan lay in the trunk, her legs pulled up to her chest and her face covered with scratches. Her hair was tousled around her and knotted strands covered her face. He brushed them away gently and her lashes fluttered over her eyes.

"Are you hurt, sweetheart?" He reached under her arms to lift her out.

"No you don't, Joshua." The male growled with a ferocity that belied the nasal tone he'd used moments ago. "She's not yours."

"She sure as hell isn't yours," Josh growled, glaring at the coyote, who opened his mouth when Josh lifted Chan out of the car.

"You don't want to do this. Chantelle won't like it when she learns who you really are," the male growled, his warning smelling stronger than his blood or the leather he wore.

Chan suddenly struggled in his arms, and Josh allowed her to slide down his body. Her clothes twisted and her nipples hardened against his chest. She dug her nails into his shoulders and every inch of him filled with a powerful need to protect her.

"Josh," she whispered, her lashes barely lifting as she turned her gaze up to him. "Get me out of here."

"Chantelle, darling." The male patted his nose with his handkerchief. "You're coming with me. I've waited a very long time for this day."

Chantelle stumbled slightly when she turned. She was hurt worse than she let on. Josh noticed she leaned against him more than she needed to. Even if she were terrified, he doubted she would be clinging to him like she was now, as if she could barely stand.

"You're going to keep on waiting." Josh lifted Chan into his arms and started toward his car.

"I paid you well for her," the male hissed behind Josh. "Both of you. Stop him."

The coyote and the male who climbed out of the car raced after Josh and grabbed him from behind. Chan fell out of his arms as he toppled backward. Her cry of pain fed his outrage when he turned on the two males. The coyote went flying across the parking lot and a quick, hard swing sent the male leopard stumbling over his own feet.

The male leopard growled fiercely. "You don't want to mess with me."

"Then leave and I won't," Josh growled, and bulldozed into him.

The two of them fell to the ground and Josh felt his clothes rip when the male extended his claws. Sharp pain sliced through his shoulder and arm. The pain pissed him off even more and he pounded the leopard underneath him with his fist. The older male standing off to the side started yelling, but Josh ignored him. Nothing he said would stop him. He wanted Chan, and not because he wanted her kept out of the asshole's stingy claws, although that was reason enough to attack. But because he wanted her.

And she wanted him. Her whispered words when he held her were enough to assure him of that. She clung to him, asking to leave. And he would get her out of here—alive.

Josh jumped to his feet, pulling the male up with him, and then threw him at the older male. "This is your only chance to get the fuck out of here," he hissed at the older male, and then turned to see Chan leaning against his car. "Get in the car," he told her.

"She won't want to leave when she knows you've lied to her." The older male's tone turned arrogant. "Tell her what your name really is, Joshua."

Josh turned slowly, staring at the older male. "Get the fuck out of here."

"It won't be that easy for you. Tell her now that you are really Joshua Pard, and not Joshua Bard."

No one knew that. Even when Josh learned the possibility that his litter once had a different name, he wasn't sure he believed it. Today, anyone who could verify or dispute it was dead. The male was insane. Joshua glared at him. "You have her attacked, try to steal her, and now insult her intelligence with lies. You've got one second to leave before you die."

"Killing me won't kill your secret." The male pulled his gaze from Josh to grumble something to the male, who then hobbled past him back to the car. "You can drive out of here with her, Joshua, but neither of you will get away. She belongs to me and always has."

"No. I don't." Chan coughed and then cleared her voice. "I don't belong to anyone. And I already know we'll get away. You're a fool and a phony if you think otherwise."

The male's smile was anything but friendly. "You're stronger than I even imagined, Chantelle, very good."

Josh was sick of this male's bullshit. He hurried over to Chan, putting his arm around her and hiding his concern when she almost completely fell against him. He held her close and opened his car door, helping her inside.

"This isn't a coyote problem anymore." The male coyote clapped his hands together and turned to his car. "We'll have our eyes on you though. If we sniff out trouble in our town, it won't be pretty."

"Don't threaten me, coyote," the male snarled. "You were paid dearly for your services."

Josh closed the car door and hated leaving Chan alone even for a moment. He walked up to the coyote, who narrowed his gaze on Josh, glancing at him sideways while slowly lowering his arms to his side. His body stiffened, his lack of trust reeking all over him.

Josh pulled his wallet out of his back pocket and yanked out the thick wad of cash the male gave him. "Here," he said, handing it all to the coyote. "Spend this on your cubs, and let your females know that leopards aren't a species to fear." He gave the male he knew had to be Leo a condemning look. "And if you ever run into problems with any of us, you contact me. I'll personally make sure they are removed and don't bother any of your dens." Josh pulled out one of his business cards and handed it to the coyote. "Thank you for bringing her to me," he said quietly.

The coyote straightened, not standing as tall as Josh, but his muscular chest and shoulders still making him appear a male to be reckoned with. "Good hunting," he said seriously.

Josh nodded. "Good hunting to you too."

"Now wait one minute." Leo walked over to them, shaking his head. His disgust was nauseating. "You're not walking out of here with all of that cash on you when I made a deal with you to turn her over to me."

The coyote shook his head, waved his hand dismissively and headed to his car. He closed the trunk and then strolled to the driver's side. Yanking his door open, he hopped in, closed it quickly and shoved the car into reverse.

"I would wish you good hunting," Josh said, taking a step toward his car and Chan. "But I doubt you've ever hunted for yourself. Try it sometime, and possibly you'll earn enough respect for those you currently hire to actually wish to remain by your side and fight with you."

"Don't judge a leopard you claim not to know." Leo watched the coyote disappear and then glanced around the empty parking lot. His gaze lingered on Josh's car behind them, but then settled on Josh's face. "But you do know me, don't you, Joshua? You fight who and what you are daily. But you know. When you let your guard down and truly search deep inside, you know damn good and well that what I'm doing is right. We'll talk soon, Joshua Pard."

Josh's claws extended before he could stop them. He snarled, wanting more than anything to kill the asshole sneering at him.

"Who are you really?" he growled, fighting the overwhelming urge to attack the male before he could answer.

"You know who I am." The male's eyes turned a pale green until they were almost clear yet still opaque. His nose was swollen and dried blood crusted above his upper lip. He ran his hand over his light almost white hair and then touched his injured face with his finger before smiling stiffly. "I'm Leo Pard, your sire."

"You didn't sire me," Josh hissed, betting it hurt like hell for the bastard to smile. "There's not enough life in you to reproduce. Watch your tail because I sure as hell will be."

Josh turned, his heart pounding furiously as he marched to his car. It took a lot of effort not to yank the door off its hinges when he pulled it open. Climbing into the closed-in space with Chan sitting there injured and smelling strongly of fear and worry, he couldn't hide his outrage quickly enough.

"Josh," she said, whimpering and reaching for him.

If he touched her, he feared he would hurt her more. He turned the key, started his car, made the wheels squeal when he spun around and got the hell out of there.

* * * * *

"Wait here." Josh looked at Chan for the first time when they pulled in to the circular drive of a small motel in St. George. "Lock the doors when I get out. I'll be able to see the car inside the lobby."

"Are you okay?" she asked, her voice hoarse.

The scratches on her face and her bloodshot eyes infuriated him further. "Fine," he said, knowing she didn't believe him. "As soon as we get a room, we'll make sure you're okay."

"Josh," she implored.

He got out of the car, moving before she could grab and keep him there. "Lock the doors," he ordered. He needed to get his outrage under control or no one would give them a room.

Josh glanced over his shoulder when he entered the lobby, noting the cars that drove down the road and those already in the parking lot. He didn't see the prick who claimed

113

to be his sire anywhere. It shouldn't have pissed him off so much that the male would spit such a horrendous lie out like that. He sucked in a slow, cleansing breath, battling his emotions as he turned his attention to the lobby. A female stood behind the counter, talking quietly on the phone. She looked at him and he tightened his insides as frustration bit at him. She was a coyote female and her guarded expression told him all he needed to know. She wasn't going to give him a room.

She hung up the phone and he noticed her hands shook before she put them out of sight beneath the counter. "I'm supposed to tell you to go over to the bed and breakfast." Her voice wavered and she straightened, lifting her head and sucking in a breath. "They'll have someone there who can help you take care of your female," she added quietly.

Josh nodded, relief flooding through him faster than he could handle. "Thank you," he said, meaning the two words more than she knew. "Good hunting."

She nodded, scribbling something on a note pad. Tearing off the piece of paper, she shoved it across the counter. "There's the address." She then turned and hurried into a back room.

Josh headed back to the car, explaining as he backed out of the stall that the coyotes were going to help them.

"They attack me and then agree to help." Chan shook her head. "This has been one hell of a day."

He read over the directions and then headed toward the bed and breakfast. Reaching for her hand, he squeezed it gently. "There are quite a few answers to figure out. But first we're going to take care of you."

She shook her head. "Get me a hot shower and I'll be fine. Nothing is broken. I'm just scratched up." She looked over at him and he glanced at her, sensing her confusion. "There were so many of them. I could have been hurt a lot worse than I was."

"What happened?" he asked.

"I slept in the canyon and woke up early." She paused as if deciding what to tell him next. When she continued, he guessed she left out a few details. "I headed out for food and they surrounded me. I couldn't get away. I remember seeing four of them in their fur, but when they attacked, suddenly there were a lot more. The last thing I remember was all of them on top of me."

He growled, his anger surfacing again at the thought of any of them touching her.

"They didn't do anything," she said quickly. "Not like you're thinking."

"What aren't you telling me?" he asked, turning into the bed and breakfast and noting how clean and private it appeared. A tall black iron fence surrounded the property, tall shrubs and evergreens practically hid the home that was set well off the road.

"This is run by coyotes?" she asked, not answering his question.

"Apparently." He parked the car, but instead of getting out, turned and studied her face. He ached to kiss every scratch, to undress her and make sure every inch of her was okay. As soon as possible, he would bathe her, make sure none of her smelled like coyotes and she was made as comfortable as possible. "Now tell me what else happened in this canyon."

She bit her lip, her eyes still bloodshot. In spite of the pain and fear that lingered on her, he smelled something else, something sweeter and more appealing. Josh smelled him on her, which he shouldn't since he hadn't come in her, yet nonetheless he swore his scent remained on her. He'd never heard of a female carrying her male's scent simply by thinking of him continuously, but maybe it was the case here. Maybe his little cat hadn't let him out of her thoughts the entire time she was away from him. Pride burst to life inside him and he covered her hand with his, ran his fingers up her arm to her face. Then brushing his finger along her jawbone, he watched her lashes flutter over her eyes.

"Tell me, Chan," he whispered.

"I possibly would have picked up on the coyotes sooner if I weren't so distracted," she said, not looking at him.

"What had you distracted?"

"You." She raised her lids, her milky green eyes swarming with desire in spite of the exhaustion he saw growing in her as her body relaxed against the seat. "I woke up wishing I hadn't made you promise you wouldn't fuck me while we were in our fur."

Josh leaned across the seat and brushed his lips over hers. "That was one of the hardest promises I've ever kept in my life," he growled.

Her eyes opened wide and she licked her lips, suddenly looking very hungry. Chan tried hard not to let him see how much pain she was in, and her strength and determination made her even more beautiful and sexy. He didn't ask, but pulled her to him, and then opened his car door, helping her out on his side.

"It meant a lot to me that you kept your word," she whispered, her voice husky. "I'll make sure I think through carefully what I ask you to promise to in the future."

More than anything he wanted to feel those full, round breasts pressed against his chest, to taste her sweet lips and breathe her sultry scent deep into his lungs. Chan had no idea how much she soothed him. Her fingers brushing down his arms, her concerned, hazy gaze searching his face, and the way her lips pressed together, forming a beautiful pouty expression hardened every inch of him and made all other matters in the world seem so incredibly trivial.

Yet it was his job right now to soothe her, take care of her until he was convinced she wasn't in pain any longer. The pain from his injured arm meant nothing to him. All that mattered was making sure Chan was comfortable. He never realized before how much of a void filled him. He ran to burn energy, snag a fresh kill, or kill time on sleepless nights. When his services were needed, he hit the road, running as a rogue male, fixing problems and then heading on his way. Not once before meeting Chan did he know that life could be like this.

He burned for her, would fight and kill for her, and would make sure no one ever harmed her again. If it meant tying her cute little body to his bed, he would do it.

"Let's get you inside," he grumbled, fighting to control the growing need that would make it damned hard to walk if he continued holding her outside where anyone might interrupt them.

"Why are we staying here?" When Chan started walking, her movements were stiff. "Why don't we hit the road and just get the hell out of here?"

Again he worried she might be hurt more so than she let on. As soon as they were in a room, he planned to get her out of those clothes and put her in a hot bath. Thoughts of joining her, running his tongue and fingers over every inch of her until he knew for himself what condition she was really in, made it hard not to simply sweep her into his arms and hurry inside, demand a room and start investigating all her sultry curves.

"Until I know beyond any doubt exactly who and what our enemies are, we're going to stay right here where everyone knows where we are, and we know where they are." He put his arm around her waist and didn't comment when she leaned against him as they climbed the stairs to the large porch.

A sign on the front door said to please enter so he pushed the door open and kept his arm around her as they walked into a dimly lit, heavily fragranced living room. Potted plants with blooming flowers that let off their perfumed scents filled the room.

Josh tightened his grip on Chan when a male about his own age walked into the room.

"You are the leopards who were sent here." The coyote didn't make it a question. His pale, almost yellow eyes moved from Josh to Chan. There were silver strands in his light brown hair, but from what Josh knew of coyotes, silver streaked their hair at maturity and not because of old age. "My mate prepared a room for you."

He turned and gestured for them to follow. They walked through a clean hallway toward a flight of stairs. A young cub stuck her head around the corner, looking at Josh and Chan with wide, curious eyes. The male growled at her and she took off running, her little feet pattering through the house even after she disappeared.

"I'm Cornelius Adrostos and my mate is Dana. We welcome you to our den."

"Josh Bard. What do we owe you?" Josh asked, deciding for the time being the less people who knew Chan's name the better.

The coyote smiled for the first time. "Your female was found in our territory unescorted. We accepted payment from the other leopard to turn the female over to him, but never agreed he would be the only leopard present when we returned her to your kind. We don't allow our females to run alone, and I apologize on behalf of my pack for the unpleasant welcome she received. When our single males take off on a run, they don't often think with the head on their shoulders. She's lucky she wasn't hurt worse than what she was." He paused, not answering the question, but opening the door and entering ahead of them as if inspecting the quarters before they could. "But Julius smelled your fear and anger when you first arrived at the gas station, which is why he confronted you. It was obvious the male offering to pay for her wasn't her mate by the way he spoke to us. We're honored to have assisted in returning her to her rightful male. Julius called and told me of your generosity when your female was returned to you. For as long as you need, our home is your sanctuary." The male coyote seemed satisfied with the quarters, placed the key on the top of the dresser next to the TV and then walked to the door. He smiled at Josh as he started closing the door. "Coyotes aren't as greedy as some might think. Julius was paid to perform a service for the leopard who took your female. He honored the terms he was contracted for. Once he smelled the dishonor in the situation, however, he backed out of the deal, and returned the money to the leopard who hired him. We take care of our own and respect other species who wish to do the same. But we also run with honor. Take care of your female and use the phone by the bed if you need anything. My mate will prepare a meal for you once it's dark. We'll call you when it's ready."

Josh swallowed the growl that tickled his throat. In spite of the coyote's generosity and friendly scent, the male made it clear that he didn't approve of Chan running alone. Well, Josh didn't either. But they were different species, and controlling a single female was harder to do than coming to terms with the fact it might be time to mate with her.

Josh made sure the door was locked and then paused, staring at the floor. Why in the hell would he even consider the thought of mating with Chan?

"This is a nice room." Chan sat on the edge of the large, king-sized bed that was in the middle of the room.

Josh snapped himself out of his odd line of thinking and looked around at the nicely furnished space. A small table in the corner had a table setting for two. There were thick curtains lining the wall and he walked over to them, opening them slightly, seeing they led out to a small deck. He noticed another door and opened it, walked into a large bathroom. A round tub, complete with jets to turn it into a whirlpool, was lined with baskets of small towels and packaged soaps. He leaned over and started the water, adjusting it until it was hot.

"And you're going to take a nice bath," he announced.

"Oh, that sounds better than perfect." She was lying down, stretched out on the large bed when he walked back into the room. "I'll be in there in a second," she murmured.

"My little cat, how badly are you hurt?" he asked, crawling over her and then moving to kneel on one side of her while unbuttoning and then unzipping her jeans. "Are these your clothes?"

She blinked slowly and then reached up to brush her hair away from her face. He noticed another scratch going down the back of her hand. Granted, leopards healed quickly and more than likely most of her cuts would be fading scars in the morning, but seeing them now, knowing males had had their fucking claws on her, made his blood boil.

"No," she said. "I was in my fur when they attacked. My clothes are on a ledge in my backpack, along with my phone and wallet. We really need to go find them." She didn't sound as if she had the energy to get up and take her bath.

Josh wanted to rip the clothes from her body, but instead focused on slowly undressing her. He almost shook from the effort it took to gently remove her clothing until she was naked beside him. "Who dressed you?" he demanded.

She shook her head slowly. "I don't know. When I came to, I was staring up at you and the others in the back of that car. It was so strange, I had a vision when we were at Birdie's nest of doing just that, of hearing that male say, "That's her, good job, we'll take her from here.""

Josh remembered Leo saying that when they stood outside the coyote's car. "What other visions have you had?"

"There was another one while I was at Birdie's. I barely remember it, but it was the same voice." Her voice grew quieter while her lashes fluttered over her eyes.

He watched her body relax as sleep consumed her. The bath would wait. His little cat needed rest. Leaving her for a moment to turn off the water, he then returned to her side and eased onto the bed so as not to wake her. The pain in his arm throbbed and he appraised his own injury while listening to her breathing grow heavier while she slipped deeper into sleep.

It wasn't clear to him how long they slept or what woke him when he blinked and stared at the ceiling in the quiet room. Chan was cuddled against him, her breathing slow and steady. He could get real accustomed to waking up with her next to him. His arm was stiff, but not in as much pain when he moved and looked at the small radio clock next to the bed.

"Is it morning?" Chan's raspy voice was filled with sleep and sounded so damned sultry he was immediately hard.

"No. We've slept for several hours though," he informed her. "How does that bath sound now?"

"Perfect," she purred.

He hated leaving her side for even a moment but stood and headed to restart the bath water. She lay on her side when he returned, the bedspread draped over her hip and only partially covering her naked body. The way her hair draped over her bare shoulder and the trusting look she gave him when he approached simply added to her beauty.

God damn. He would kill to protect this female—*his* female.

Josh slid his arm underneath her, lifting her into his arms and off the bed. Her skin was like satin against his arms and she relaxed when he lifted her, resting her head next to his shoulder. He carried her into the bathroom where the large tub was slowly filling with steamy hot water.

"That looks so good," she muttered, her voice a lazy drawl.

He let her slide down his body, feeling her hard nipples move across his chest and her slender, petite body rubbing against his until she stood. There were a few fading bruises and several scratches on her legs. But he didn't see anything that looked as if she'd been mauled or beaten, which matched the story the coyote told him. Nonetheless, he wanted to inspect her in detail, very close and careful detail.

"Before we fell asleep you mentioned another vision? Do you remember what happened in it?" he asked, kneeling before the tub and testing the water. He then grabbed one of the soaps and unwrapped it. There were small bottles of shampoo and conditioner on the bathroom counter and he brought these to the edge of the tub. "Get in," he ordered.

"All he said was, 'Does any of this look familiar?', or something like that," she said, taking his hand and stepping into the water. "Oh Josh, this is heaven," she purred, and smiled up at him as she reclined in the water.

"Looks better than heaven," he growled, staring down at her body as the water washed over her belly and breasts. Her nipples were hard and puckered. Her legs spread just enough for him to see her sweet pussy before the water rushed over it. "And what looked familiar?"

Her hair was wet from the shoulders down and stuck to her body, molding over her perfectly round, full breasts. "I don't remember," she said softly, shaking her head and bending her knees as she sank deeper into the tub.

Josh started removing his clothes, studying her as her lids grew heavy and finally closed. She hummed softly, lazily lifting her cupped hand and pouring water over her body. When he was naked, he stepped into the water and then moved her so he could sit behind her in the tub. She blinked quickly, looking up at him as if he just woke her.

"How are you feeling?" he asked.

"A bit stiff, but I'm okay," she uttered, her gaze dropping to his hard cock. "What are you going to do?"

"I'm going to bathe you, clean every inch of your body until I'm convinced there is no smell of coyotes on you."

"Do I smell like coyotes?"

"No, my little cat. You smell like you're dying to be fucked. Would you like me to make you another promise?"

"What?" She turned her head, nibbling her lower lip while glancing over her shoulder at him as he adjusted himself behind her. "What promise would that be?"

"I promise that I'm going to do everything to you I ached to do to you the other night and couldn't because I swore I wouldn't."

Chapter Nine

ೞ

Hot water poured into the tub, filling it slowly. Josh sat behind her and the water swelled, covering her smoldering flesh. His hard, muscular body with a perfect sprinkle of hair over his chest, pressed against her backside. A fever exploded inside her that had nothing to do with her injuries. In fact, the more aware she was of him, the less her body hurt. At least it didn't hurt from any injury.

"I take it by your scent that you approve of my promise," he growled into her ear, his hands moving over her breasts and then squeezing.

She closed her eyes and let her head fall back against his shoulder. "Yes," she said, smiling slowly. "You may clean me."

He pinched her nipples, squeezing and pulling at the same time. Charged bolts of electricity shot hard and fast down her middle and straight to her clit.

"Oh shit," she hissed, biting her lip hard enough to taste blood. The metallic taste in her mouth fueled her craving and made her insides throb.

His heart pounded against her back. His cock lengthened, sliding over her lower back when she shifted in the water.

"My little cat wishes to be cleaned," he said, his voice hoarse and gravelly. "Then she will be. And I take any job I do very seriously."

She wanted to tell him to put his hands back on her breasts when he let go. But he straightened behind her in the water. He lifted her hair, pulling it together until he held most of it at her nape.

"Cleaning me was your idea." She relaxed, rolling her head when he pulled and gathered the rest of her hair. "Not that I'm complaining."

"Complaining wouldn't be to your advantage right now," he informed her, and then placed his free hand in the water and over her hip. "Slide into the water so we can get all of your hair wet. First your hair and then your body."

He was going to torture her. His hard cock brushed against her ass and then her back, letting her feel his arousal. Yet his voice was so smooth, so in control. He touched her with confidence, never hesitating. While she was flustered, slowly drowning with the smell and sensations pounding inside her from her own lust, he was a brick wall of determination.

Which was damned unfair.

"Slip into the water. Get all of your hair wet," he instructed again, pushing against her body so she would slide forward. He continued holding her while moving her body until she lay between his legs. "That's my good little cat," he purred, his deep baritone gliding over her flesh just as his fingers did, escalating the feverish torment inside her. "Your hair is so thick, so beautiful."

She actually purred. Chan couldn't remember the last time something gave her so much pleasure that she purred out loud. There wasn't any controlling the rumbling in her throat when his fingers massaged her head. Then cradling her with one hand, he managed the small bottle and poured the shampoo over her hair.

"Rinse," he ordered, again holding her firmly and dunking her into the water so he was able to comb the soap from her hair.

He repeated the process with the conditioner, massaging it into her thick, long hair with steady, skilled fingers that offered so much pleasure she wasn't sure she would live through the experience.

"You've missed your calling in life," she muttered, feeling so relaxed and enjoying how the hot water covered her body and how his hands manipulated her so she lay exactly where he wanted her. "That feels so wonderful."

"I'm not done yet," he promised, the dark sensuality in his tone making her insides flutter. "Sit up."

"You better not be done yet." She felt the tender spots on her body from being attacked by the coyotes for the first time when she moved in the water. Josh hadn't said anything about the scratches on her face, and she knew they would heal quickly, but when he turned her so she now leaned against his bent leg, she lowered her face so her wet hair fell forward and shielded her from his view.

Josh chuckled softly. "You have no problem being spoiled, do you?"

"Is that what you're doing?" She blinked water from her eyes and raised her hand to touch her face. The memory of the coyotes jumping at her appeared against her will when she brushed her fingers over her bruised cheekbone and flinched.

"You should know what it's like to be spoiled, Chan," he said, and then brushed her hair behind her shoulder. "Look at me."

She did, frustration and stubbornness taking over. And it irritated her. "I'm sure I do as much as you do," she said, instantly hating the hurt she heard in her tone. She didn't want this moment ruined with any realities. He was making her feel so damned good. Why couldn't she just let go and enjoy it?

Noticing the bruising on his arm, she touched it with her fingertips. "Are you okay?" He'd endured injuries fighting for her.

"I'm fine," he said. "I want you to make me a promise." He held her chin, taking his time studying her face, tilting it slightly as he examined in detail every one of her injuries.

Chan closed her eyes, the throbbing between her legs just as intense as it had been since he first carried her into the bathroom. And his cock, now brushing against the curve of her hip, swelled into a fierce hardness that she ached to have buried inside her.

"What's that?" In spite of her feverish need, of the way her flesh tingled wherever he touched her, a growing lump in her gut created growing uneasiness inside her.

"I want your word that you'll never run from me again."

She opened her eyes, her breath catching in her chest and swelling painfully when she saw how intense his expression was. Josh's eyes glowed with something that bordered on dangerous. He let go of her face and reached for the washcloth and soap.

"Swear to me, Chan," he said, looking away and focusing on the task of lathering the cloth.

Suddenly the vision she'd had while at Birdie's reappeared in her mind. She saw herself standing, leaning against him, as if she hovered over herself and Josh.

"I love you," she heard herself say.

The image disappeared and she found herself watching the white bubbly suds ooze over his fingers and down his wrist. Focusing on the hairline scratch stretching over the bruise on his arm, she accepted that he'd fight for her. Which meant he had honor. But if he were a hunter, a leopard willing to race from city to city helping anyone who needed him, he would display honor to many. A commendable trait but not necessarily proof that he felt anything stronger for her other than determination to protect her from an insane leopard. How would they get from where they were now to the moment when she would so casually say that to him?

"I can't," she began.

He grabbed her arm, pinching her skin, and pressed the soapy washcloth to her chest, just above her breasts.

"You can and you will," he demanded.

"Josh." She shook her head, hating the pain that was eating up the desire still torturing her insides. "Just because we see things, minute images of what will happen at some point in time in the future, doesn't mean we know when it will happen between us. If things were to change…"

Even as she spoke, she couldn't imagine wanting him out of her life. But being a realist kept her alive.

"Swear to me, Chantelle. Because if you don't, I'm going to chain you to my side until you do, damn it. I want your word now."

"I will give you my word that as long as you don't do something that infuriates me, or puts me in danger…"

"I would never fucking put you in danger," he growled.

And she believed him. He rubbed the cloth over her shoulder, being surprisingly gentle considering the anger that quickly hardened his expression.

"You will promise me," he said, speaking slow and soft while focusing on her body as he rubbed the cloth over her breasts, driving her crazy as the washcloth suddenly seemed a lot rougher than it had a moment before when it brushed over her nipples. "If I infuriate you, annoy you in any way, or even push you to the point where you feel the urge to run like you did before, talk to me about it before you leave."

"Okay," she whispered, her voice suddenly failing her.

The swelling discomfort lodged in her gut quickly moved to her chest and swelled around her heart, constricting to the point that it hurt so bad she feared she might cry. Josh looked up at her with such a pained, tortured expression that she pulled her hand out of the water, reached for him before she gave it any thought. His muscles twitched under her touch, but he didn't look away.

"I didn't run from you."

"Oh really," he muttered, dipping the cloth in the water and then rinsing the soap from her shoulders and breasts.

"Jin Rose came to the room."

The glazed look in his eyes disappeared so quickly she wasn't sure it was ever there. Although she would swear that for those brief moments she saw raw pain surface inside him, it suddenly was replaced with a clear, hard expression.

"She did, did she? What did she want? Why didn't you tell me?"

"She told me that Leo Pard was intent on having me, obsessed, although she denied it was an obsession. I insulted him, told her his methods showed his lack of character and honor, but she was determined to sell him to me. She told me his desire to have me was so strong that..."

"That what?" he growled, jerking her arm and then letting go of it. He re-lathered the washcloth and tenderly started wiping it over the scratches on her face.

Chan closed her eyes. "I'm confusing what she said with what I felt," she admitted, and realized at the same moment that she'd never talked like this to another leopard before.

"Tell me exactly what she said." He dabbed gingerly at her face.

She grabbed his wrist, not wanting him to nurture her, or treat her like someone who needed tended to and cared for. It made it too damned hard to think straight, keep her wits about her and her sense of self-control. When she pushed against his wrist, he easily took her hand with his other and removed her grip from his wrist. Then he continued wiping her face.

"She told me that she sought me out to tell me to run, to leave before Leo showed up and to disappear, go where no one would find me," she spit out, speaking quickly and then closing her mouth when he rinsed the cloth and brought it to her face again to wipe off the soap.

"And you couldn't come talk to me about this?" He sounded angry again, but she couldn't see with the cloth covering her face.

She waited until he finished. Josh turned her again, this time so her back was to the water that continued to pour hot from the tap. The tub was almost full now and water sloshed around her. She pushed her palms against the bottom of the tub and stabilized herself. Josh moved his legs, the hair on his thighs brushing against hers and heightening her senses drastically. He straightened and then pulled her closer to him so she sat almost cross-legged in between his legs. Once again, ignoring the intimacy of their positioning, he focused on the task of lathering his cloth.

Chan grabbed her hair, twisting the water from it and then pushing it over her shoulder. Her gaze rested on his cock, which jutted up toward her under the water. If she relaxed her hands in front of her, they would drift down and touch him. The thought she could do that made her heart pitter-patter with nervous excitement. She didn't want to dampen the mood again with such serious conversation. It was pointless to discuss what had already happened. It wouldn't change any of the facts.

"There were leopards everywhere and it would raise suspicion if I approached you and told you I was leaving. I waited for Jin to go downstairs and then packed and took off. I didn't even go in the direction she suggested, instead purchased a ticket to Phoenix."

"I know," he said sardonically. "I would say your smartest move was getting off the bus before you arrived at your destination. But none of it was smart."

"I should have just waited for him to show up and take me?" she demanded.

"I wouldn't have let that happen, any more than I let him take you earlier today," he snapped. "You ran and were attacked. Damn it, Chan, they could have raped you, each and every one of those coyotes. They could have taken turns fucking you. And what if when they were done they simply left you? What then? You could have died."

"It didn't happen like that."

"And you're damned lucky that it didn't."

"What do you want me to say?" she cried out, suddenly shaking with her own frustration over the accuracy of the words and hating the fact she hadn't been able to defend herself from the coyotes. "If that many coyotes attacked you, the same thing would have happened. Maybe they wouldn't rape you. But you try and make me believe a strong healthy male could have warded off that many coyotes in an ambush. Anyone attacked like that, with those odds, would have gone down. And I'm fucking fine."

"God damn it, Chan." He dropped the cloth in the water and grabbed her arms, dragging her up against his chest. His arms wrapped around her with such aggressiveness that she collapsed against him, the water and positioning making it impossible to push away from him. He grabbed the back of her hair, holding her face where he wanted it, and devoured her mouth.

She cried into the kiss, trying to raise her arms and wrap them around him. He impaled her mouth, demanding so much as he thrust deep inside her. His tongue swirled around hers, drinking and taking, filling her with heat that sent the smoldering need inside her quickly to the boiling point.

He growled, moving his hands roughly down her side, allowing her just a bit of freedom to drag her fingers over the perfectly carved muscles in his chest. He was so warm, so hard and solid. She felt muscles shift under her fingertips and his heart beat with confident strength as she explored.

Josh bit at her lip and then pulled on her hair, forcing her head to fall back as he created a path of hot, sensual kisses and nips down her neck and then to her breasts. He moved over her, coming up out of the water and cradling her with one arm while leaning her back. Gliding her across the tub, he pressed her against the side of it, so she was able to lean her head against the edge.

Chan spread her legs, the heat inside her burning with furious anticipation. She grabbed his shoulders, aching to have him inside her more than she wanted to breathe. All of the promises and discussions of what ifs weren't going to get them anywhere. No matter how much she'd thought about him from the moment she left him, too much bullshit was going on around them to think beyond it. They needed to figure out why some strange male wanted her so badly. She wanted to know why the coyotes would take payment to turn her over to Leo Pard, but then bring Josh to the rendezvous point. Did they detect the insanity in his scent when they talked to him? She was too out of it when Pard was present to detect anything from him. It was a mystery, and it was getting more and more personal every day.

Besides, dwelling on the possibilities that something stronger than lust existed between her and Josh was almost as terrifying as realizing she was being stalked. For the time being, the two of them were in this together. And so okay, she'd lusted after him big time when she woke up this morning, and after her nap. Getting up close and personal sexually was the perfect diversion. It would allow her time to clear her head, ease the craving that was out of control inside her, but she couldn't risk letting it go beyond that. If she gave him her heart, she could get hurt worse than anything the coyotes could do to her. She would give him her body and enjoy the hell out of his. But that was it.

Grabbing his non-injured shoulder, Chan kept herself braced in the water while spreading her legs and pressing her feet against the opposite side. Josh reached for the faucet, turning the water off, and then pushed the button on the side of the tub. Instantly the jets came to life, creating bubbles everywhere as the water started circulating and brushing over her already feverish skin. It hit her lower back, massaging and causing even more sensations to rush over her, through her, until her insides swelled with an imminent explosion.

"You should see your face," he whispered, and then scraped her earlobe with his teeth.

Chills rushed over her so aggressively she arched into them, feeling the sensation of his nibbling clear down to her toes. "Don't look at it if you don't like it," she mumbled, keeping her eyes closed, enjoying the hell out of how his body felt brushing over hers.

"Oh, I like it. I like it very much," he growled. "The way your cheeks flush when you're so close to coming. Perfection."

She scraped her lip with her teeth. It was as if she couldn't catch her breath. Josh licked and nipped his way down her neck and then hit that tender spot just above her collarbone, making her jump.

"You're so close, Chan," he whispered against her flesh. "When I enter you, you're going to come."

She opened her eyes, so close to panting, and told herself she wouldn't let herself get that out of control. Josh reached under her arms, lifting her in the water. She let her hands slide down his shoulders and grabbed his arms.

"Look at the water dripping off of your nipples."

She looked down just as he lapped at her nipple with his tongue. Then, looking up at her, he closed his teeth over her puckered flesh and pulled.

"Shit," she hissed.

He growled, sounding very satisfied with the torture he inflicted on her. Chan dug her fingers into his muscles, holding on tight while he flicked at her nipple with his tongue and held it between his teeth.

"God that feels good." She never would have guessed she liked her nipple being nibbled on. But every time he closed his teeth against it and the pain hit just hard enough to send streaks of electricity bolting through her, her pussy clenched. And in spite of being in the rushing water, she could feel the cream clinging to her folds.

Even with the jets forcing the water to rush against her body, the smell of her desire was intoxicating. And it wasn't just her that she smelled. Josh's lust swarmed around her. Beads of water trickled down his chest, and she imagined they carried his aromatic lustful scent with them.

She adjusted her legs, wrapping them around him, and could feel his hard cock pressing against her in the water. It brushed against her rear-end then moved, poking her inner thigh.

Josh sucked her nipple into his mouth, tugging on it like a starving cub. His fingers rubbed her sides, caressing and gliding over her until he cupped her breasts. She loved the attention, the incredible detail he offered while adoring her body. Chan leaned into him, pressing her breasts into his face and then dragged her nails up his arms, down his back.

He growled his approval and corded muscle twitched and shifted as she explored with her hands. God. He made her feel so fucking good. And with the water rushing around them, massaging her back, she could so easily melt into a wonderful state of bliss.

How incredible it would be to simply let go and enjoy all of this without any of the worries plaguing the back of her brain. Steam tumbled around her in the air, and his hard-packed body was warm and so damned perfect. Every sensation she experienced offered so much pleasure and such a tempting invitation to give in and surrender. Josh made her feel so wonderful. All he asked was a commitment from her to allow him to offer protection. Maybe just for a few she would allow herself to believe all of this could last forever.

The only thing she couldn't fathom was complete submission. She wanted control, including knowing Josh would be there when she needed him. But controlling her, demanding she promise never to leave his side without his consent? It wasn't going to happen. Any more than she would tolerate waiting until he decided he'd tortured her enough before he fucked her.

She dug her fingernails into the hard muscles of his back and then dragged them up along his spine. Josh's growl turned into a rumble that vibrated throughout his body as he slowly let go of her breast and arched into her own personal torture session. His eyes were a deep, intense green that was almost the shade of emeralds. He met her gaze, his hair damp with curls forming around his face and neck.

"It's time for you to pay attention to other parts of my body," she purred, smiling when his expression darkened. "Does my big bad cat not know how to take orders?" she growled, dragging her fingers over his non-injured shoulder, up the sides of his neck and into his hair.

She pulled hard and Josh let out a ferocious growl, grabbing her wrists and trying to yank her hands from his hair. She rubbed her breasts against his wet chest, loving how his hair scratched her nipples and ignited even more fire inside her. Taking the moment and holding on to his hair as he pulled her hands from his head, she glided down him and on to his rock-hard cock.

Her pussy was inflamed and the rich aroma of her arousal spilled into the steam when his cock rubbed against her swollen entrance.

"Fuck me now," she growled, clenching her teeth together and putting some strength into it to push against the power he exerted.

"You think you can tell me what to do?" he snarled, squeezing her wrists hard enough to push her bones together.

The stinging sensation wasn't as painful as it was exhilarating and she pushed herself down onto his cock, managing to bring him halfway inside her before he could stop her efforts. Even then, with him partially entered, the glaze that quickly covered his dilated pupils told her she had him.

"Oh darling," she purred, lowering her voice to a sultry whisper. "I know that I can."

Josh moved quickly. Letting go of her wrists gave her free rein to tangle her fingers through his thick, wet curls, but she barely had time to brush her fingertips over his head. Josh grabbed her hips and stood. Water splashed around them, spraying the air and stirring the hot steam that whirled around them. He pushed her back against the shower wall, thrusting inside her with so much aggression she swore he split her in two.

At that moment she wished they weren't in a coyote's den, in a room graciously offered to them on the grounds that she could convalesce better. Chan bit her lip so she wouldn't howl, although she wanted to scream, and tossed her head back hard enough it hit the wall behind her. Josh continued thrusting, impaling her again and again while his expression turned fierce with determination.

If he thought he gained her submission by fucking her harder than she'd ever been taken in her life, she would just let him think that. He gave her exactly what she wanted, what she demanded, and she held on for dear life, sliding over the edge and coming again and again.

"I told you, you would come when I entered you," he said through gritted teeth, barely moving his mouth. His wet curls fell around his face, adding to the roguish look she found so sexy about him.

"Intelligence is a good quality in a male," she said in between gasps. "As is obedience," she added softly, offering a coy smile and batting her eyelashes as she stared into his intense eyes.

"Chan," he growled, pushing her harder against the wall and driving his cock deeper into her. "You're going to drain me. Shit," he hissed before crushing her with his body as his muscles started jerking.

His head collapsed against her shoulder and she wrapped her arms tight around his neck, holding him as he spilled his come deep inside her.

"God damn," he whispered, his body jerking while his cock twitched repeatedly.

The water continued swirling around their legs. It forced the steam to tumble over them. Her hair clung to her face and neck, and his heavy breathing matched hers while the thick fog of lust hung heavy around them. She loved the way their scents mixed together, creating an aroma that was almost sweet yet musky at the same time.

When the scent didn't fade, but the fog in her brain did, a slow fact slowly surfaced. Josh just came inside her. It was a damn good thing she enjoyed the way they smelled together, because that rich fragrance would cling to her, remaining strong enough for others to notice.

Josh had just marked her as his female. She wasn't in heat, or close to it, so getting pregnant wasn't a problem. But unless she left him, didn't fuck him again and quit thinking about him, his scent on her wouldn't fade. The rest of the world would view them as mated.

Chapter Ten

The backyard of the bed and breakfast was a private sanctuary just like the rest of the place. Someone had invested some money in landscaping the property just right. Trees, shrubs and vines created natural walls that would make it difficult for anyone to approach without being noticed. Josh glanced back at the house while pulling his cell phone out and flipping it open. He entered a number, let the phone ring twice and then hung up.

He wouldn't allow things to settle too much before touching base with his cousin. Thad would keep his nose to the ground, and if anything new brewed, his cousin would catch wind to it. Josh and Chan might just have each other through this nightmare, but Thad would serve as a trustworthy contact. He was younger, and the less involved he was in all of this, the better Josh felt, but it was necessary to have someone out there watching the others' tails for them.

Chan opened the back door and stepped outside just as he clipped his phone to his belt.

"What are you doing?" she asked, her hair freshly brushed and the scratches on her face almost completely faded. A good night's sleep and incredible sex made her glow this morning. "Did you get some food?"

"Yes. Cornelius' mate is a wonderful cook."

"Dana is a good cook," she said, watching her bare feet as she walked silently along a stone path to an old, heavy-looking stone bench. She sat and pressed her palms flat against the seat on either side of her, still focusing on her feet. "So what are you doing out here?" she asked again.

"I'm waiting on a phone call." His scent was buried deep in her. The way it drifted in the air, mixing with her own sweet aroma, smelled so damned good he was hard instantly.

Chan looked up quickly, her long hair drifting over her shoulders and her mouth forming a small, adorable circle. "Oh," she said, and pushed off the bench. "I'll leave you to your privacy then. I just wanted to say one thing though. I gave my word not to run again."

Instantly he stiffened. "What?" he growled, grabbing her arm and then moving her hair so he could see her face.

"I need my things. I'm sure I can find the ledge I slept on the other night. At the least I'd like some of my clothes and my phone and wallet." She moved and put her hand over his, pulling him off her arm and then walking down the path away from him. "I don't even have my makeup bag or nail polish or anything. I know going to my home probably isn't too smart right now."

"You're damned straight." He came up on her then turned her around to face him. "Cornelius sent one of the members of his pack to retrieve your things. They are inside and you can make sure everything that is yours is there. We'll buy you some new clothes, but returning to your apartment right now isn't a smart move. There are too many humans around and I won't allow a leopard attack to happen in the middle of such a large human city."

She nodded once, her lips pressed together in a firm line. "Agreeing to talk to you wasn't an agreement to do as you say," she said flatly. "I'm not comfortable among coyotes. Cornelius and Dana are being very nice, but they aren't comfortable with us being here either. They keep their cubs away from me." She shook her head and then crossed her arms over her chest, pushing her breasts together so that even with the sweater she wore, the plump flesh pressed against the material and grabbed his attention. "But it's more than that," she added, searching his face. "I'm not going to live my life on the run. Whatever these leopards want, I'd rather face it than turn tail and hide."

"We're hardly hiding." In fact, he was about ready to blast their presence into the bastard's face. "I'm sure Leo knows exactly where we are. He's not going to come..."

"Leo," she hissed, narrowing her gaze on him.

She moved her hands to her hips, glaring at him and forcing her scent to hang even heavier in the air between them. In spite of her spicy-smelling anger, the erotic aroma of her scent mixed with his appealed to him more than he guessed it would.

"Leo, as in Leo Pard," she demanded, her voice growing shriller with each word. "He's the one I've seen in my visions. Who the hell is he?"

"I met him for the first time yesterday."

Her anger didn't subside. But her hardened expression softened, her features relaxing as her milky green eyes suddenly got a faraway look about them. Her lips parted and her tongue appeared, moistening her lips while her hands slowly lowered to her sides. As quickly as her emotions drained from her, they returned, and her attention snapped back to him. She didn't say anything although her mouth opened to speak. She then looked down, as if something confused her.

"What? You just had another vision." He'd never met another leopard who had visions like he did, but even then, Chan seemed to have them a lot more often. "Chan," he pressed. If she were around the wrong leopards and a vision hit her, it would be obvious. A protector's instinct kicked in so hard it was like a vicious punch to his gut.

Her visions left her vulnerable, her defenses down momentarily. He saw it in the confused look she gave him before she regained her composure and the sharpness returned to her pretty green eyes.

"Come back over here and sit down," he said, softening his tone and rubbing her shoulder as he tried guiding her to the stone bench.

Chan stiffened, her defiance returning with a rush that almost cooled the air around them. "Don't patronize me, Josh. I'm fine and don't need to be treated like a cub."

"There's a difference between insulting you and caring about you."

Her eyes widened and she looked up at him then wrapped her arms around herself and marched back to the bench. She didn't sit though. Instead, turning on him sharply, she gave him a piercing stare.

"Who are you really?" she demanded. "I might have just regained consciousness in the back of that car, but other than being out of it, I wasn't hurt that bad. And I heard what that male—that Leo Pard—said to you."

His cell phone started vibrating at his waist but he ignored it. If he lost her trust, he lost everything. That wasn't something he would risk. Chan carried his scent, something he was damned proud of. Her willful, stubborn and defiant nature appealed to him as much as her sexy curves, her long, thick wavy hair, and the way she glared at him, hiding her pain because she feared he'd deceived her.

All that mattered right now was she trust him enough to believe him over some pansy-ass prick who was a humiliation to his species. Someday he would learn how Leo Pard discovered a secret that was over twenty years old. And one that had no bearing on who he was today. "I'm Joshua Bard. My den is in Wheeler's Point, a small town on Lake of the Woods. My parents aren't alive anymore but I have two littermates. We don't talk much, which is my fault, not theirs. I also have a cousin, the only cub from my mother's littermate. His name is Thad Pierce, and he's also a hunter. I trained him myself."

She nodded, frowning. "Leo Pard said he was your sire," she said, looking down at her hands and seeming incredibly interested in her fingernails all of a sudden. "He said I wouldn't be so impressed by you once I learned you were lying."

"Do you smell lies on me?"

She shook her head slowly and when she looked up, the pain that clouded her pretty eyes was even stronger. "Some leopards are incredibly good at hiding the smell of lies," she whispered.

"God damn it," he growled, turning from her when the urge to hit something — hard — almost overwhelmed him. He faced her and blew out an exasperated sigh when she looked at him warily. "I'll kill that bastard for planting doubt in you, Chan. I have no idea why he said that. Desperation maybe? He wants you, and I have you. He spit out vicious lies. But none of them are true. My sire was a Bard. That much I could prove to you."

She searched his face and her expression relaxed. "I believe you."

He released a relieved sigh and pulled her into his arms. "That means more to me than you know," he whispered into her hair.

His phone buzzed again and Chan pulled away from him. She watched as he pulled it from his belt. "I'll leave if that's your phone call."

"No." He wanted to give her satisfaction that he wasn't hiding anything from her. "Sit down and listen. When I'm done with my call you can tell me what you just saw."

She sat, crossing her narrow ankles over each other and wiggling her toes. "It was the same male I saw the other times in my visions and who was with you yesterday when I came to in the trunk of the car. I guess it's Leo Pard. He said I shouldn't trust you."

"You shouldn't trust him," he said firmly. Then flipping his phone open, he accepted the call. "Thad?"

"Yeah," Thad said on the other end. "All cool with you?"

"At the moment," he told his cousin. "I'm with Chan and we're staying at a bed and breakfast in St. George, Utah. It's run by coyotes but they seem to be taking a neutral stand at the moment."

"I would too if I could." Thad chuckled dryly. "I've gone north. It might be smart if you did the same. We're stronger on our home turf."

"It crossed my mind. I'll see if I can talk Chan into it."

"Chan? Chantelle Drap?" Thad asked. "You getting cozy?"

"Yup." He watched Chan search his face, guessing she could hear his cousin through the phone. Cell phones had their advantages, but a strong disadvantage was that a caller practically had to whisper to keep everyone on the other end of the line from hearing them. "What have you learned about the other hunters? And this Leo character. Who the hell is he?"

"I traced the ISP that posted on the PI website to a location outside of Phoenix." Thad was the computer geek, and if there were any dirt to find on anyone, he'd sniff it out. "It's a small town, Fountain Hills. Race Ogden will run with us. He doesn't have an agenda, and as far as I can tell from what I've found on him, he keeps his tail clean. I'm not so sure about Tore Mann. He runs a bit more on the wild side and I say we leave him out. Jin Rose is another ghost."

"A ghost? What do you mean?" He watched Chan frown as he asked and cock her head as if trying to listen better.

"I can't find anything on her, not where she's from or who her litter is—nothing."

"Interesting." He wasn't sure any of the hunters other than his cousin could be trusted right now. It wasn't uncommon for hunters to keep a low profile, not mate and remain aloof. His sire had shared stories of his adventures prior to mating, but a lot of them weren't as clear in Josh's memory, especially after his sire's untimely death.

But assuring Chan's safety and that the two of them could attempt living normal lives meant they needed to know who their enemies were and where they were. "Keep searching. We'll be in touch soon. I'm going to take a hot little female out to buy polish for her nails."

"Crap. You're a fucking goner."

"Might be." Josh grinned at Chan's scowling expression as he hung up the phone. "Let's go, darling."

* * * * * *

It always amazed Josh how buying new things, especially little items like soap, hand lotion and makeup, could transform a woman's mood. There wasn't much to pack up at the bed and breakfast, which made it easy to appear as if they were simply going shopping and would return later. Their shopping excursion included purchasing clothes for both of them, new suitcases, the feminine items Chan needed, and new bras and panties that he enjoyed helping her pick out. He waited until they were on the road for a few hours before calling Cornelius Adrostos and telling him they wouldn't be returning.

His car got fairly good mileage and he was damned glad he'd filled up when he first arrived in St. George. But driving north and keeping off the major interstates so he could better watch to see if they were followed meant slowing when they hit small towns and pushing his car when they hit higher elevations. Nonetheless, they made it a good five hours before he finally stopped to fill his tank again. It was tempting to stop and nap as the hours passed by and darkness surrounded them. Chan slept soundly next to him, curled up on her side with her long, blonde hair streaming past her shoulders and over her breasts.

He loved her relaxed expression when she slept. The more time they spent together the easier it was to read and understand her moods. Chan was determined not to appear weak to him, but her vulnerable side added to her sex appeal. And right now, with her breathing softly next to him, his scent still embedded in her flesh, it was all he could do to keep his hands on the wheel and not reach over and stroke her enticing curves.

Turning his attention to the two-lane road that twisted like a black snake in front of him, his conversation with Chan came to mind. He ached to break Leo Pard's neck for spouting ridiculous lies. If his sire were still alive he would fight Josh for the right to do the damage.

Memories slowly surfaced he hadn't given thought to in years. In spite of his efforts to shove them out of his head, there wasn't much else to think about as the hours drifted by slowly and the road continued curving and twisting endlessly.

He had been barely ten, a cub enjoying fighting and racing with the other cubs in his neighborhood. The day his life ended appeared in his brain with such clarity he experienced a moment of panic that he might be witnessing a vision while driving. The road didn't disappear though, or the ridges of the steering wheel against his fingers. Nonetheless, he still saw the day his parents died, and his life as a happy, carefree cub ended.

They were running, flying over the open land around the lake. He still remembered how round the moon was, how it glowed bright. His sire ran ahead, his mother and littermates around him. Josh almost opened his mouth, just as he did during that run when he lunged and nipped at his brother playfully. It was at that minute they appeared. Maybe if he weren't busy attacking his littermate he could have saved his sire.

Just as it happened twenty years ago, Josh swore the hard ground tore at his side. He rolled his littermate over and his younger brother leaped on top of both of them. They tumbled down the bank, falling into the black water and then immediately howling and scrambling to get out of the freezing water.

Josh climbed out and shook the water out of his coat furiously. At first he saw blurs, large dark objects bounding toward them too quickly for him to register any type of reaction. He didn't howl. He didn't attack. All he did was stand by the lake, water dripping from his coat as the leopards attacked his sire.

It was his mother's scream that kick-started his brain and forced him to move. And then all he did was race to her side like a fucking helpless, terrified cub. His littermates rammed into him, clawing and yelping like helpless babies.

Josh gripped the steering wheel hard enough to hurt his hands. He ground his teeth, feeling them grow and pinch his gums. It tore at his pride as badly as it ripped his heart out that he'd screamed the loudest. Begging for protection from their mother while she struggled against her own cubs to try to save her mate. But there were too many of them. Leopards he didn't recognize, was positive he'd never seen before, attacked and killed his sire and then went after his mother.

Josh squeezed his eyes shut just for a moment, demanding the memory to disappear. He glanced over at Chan, who had pulled her legs up to her chest and hunched over so she slept curled in a ball on the seat next to him. He reached for her, needing to touch her, to pull his mind back to the present and get his ugly, disgusting past to go the fuck away.

He stroked her hair, the smoothness of it soothing his burning palm after having gripped the wheel too hard. She purred, stretching and moving so she fell toward him. He moved his hand to her back, encouraging her to lay her head on his lap.

"You're safe," he whispered, glancing down at her and then back at the road. "No one will ever hurt you while you're with me."

Never again. He wasn't a fucking cub anymore. They'd destroyed his parents, ruined his life. But this time he knew how to fight back, and he knew how to kill. Leo Pard called forth the hunters. Maybe some of them could be bought, but Josh took the ancient trade of protecting his species very seriously. And he took protecting Chan even more so.

Josh stroked Chan's hair, relaxing his hand on the steering wheel when finally the ghastly images of his past disappeared back into the dark corners of his brain. One puzzle still remained. Who the hell was Leo Pard? Glancing down at Chan, he silently promised her he would destroy the bastard before the fucking prick destroyed them.

* * * * *

"Please tell me we aren't going to meet anyone right away." Chan shifted in her seat, dragging her fingers through her hair as she struggled to look in the small mirror behind the visor. "I look like crap and would kill for a shower."

"I didn't tell anyone we were coming here." Josh turned onto the one-lane gravel road and slowed, noting the owls in the trees as they drove by. They took flight after he drove by and he guessed taking refuge in his cabin wouldn't be a secret for long.

Chan glanced over her shoulder. "Those were owls," she reported, turning quickly to look at him.

"Owls are thick around here, but not foes. The worst they'll do is tell Thad we're here and you'll get that reception you don't want." He was exhausted as hell and had half a mind to ignore anyone who came sniffing around until he could crash for at least a good eight hours.

"Is that how you know Birdie?" she asked, once again trying to comb the knots out of her hair.

"He's been out this way a couple of times. But we met down in Phoenix too."

The old cabin was just as he remembered it. Pulling his car to a stop outside the front door, he cut the engine and then climbed out slowly. That shower Chan wanted sounded real damned good.

"Damn," Chan whispered on a breath as she climbed out on her side and stretched.

He thought she didn't like it until he glanced over the roof of the car and saw her staring at the cabin. Her cheeks flushed from the harsh, cold air, and her nipples puckered to eager points against the new sweater that hugged her slender figure. Chan glanced around at the rugged land surrounding them and then raised her arms over her head, clasping them together, stretching. It might have been thirty degrees outside, but suddenly it felt like eighty. He became hard as a rock and simply stared, enjoying the best damned view there was.

She turned and grinned at him, oblivious to how she affected him. "This place is awesome."

"It will take some work winterizing it." His parents had brought him here when he was a cub, and returning without them wasn't the same. "I figured we'd be left alone here, which will give us time to learn more about what is going on."

After hauling their new suitcases, filled with their new clothes, into the cabin, Chan started exploring while he inspected the fireplace. He successfully worked the kinks out of his body chopping fresh firewood and then making sure the chimney was free of rodents and their nests. He fired up the hot water heater and inspected the outside of the cabin and roof. It had been years since he'd been here and the place was still in good shape. Someone had taken good care of it over the years, and he guessed Thad made use of the place from time to time.

Josh was surprised to feel heat when he walked back inside. Chan already had a fire going, making quick use of the wood he'd cut. Obviously she'd found the small washer and dryer because the machines hummed in the hallway. He walked into the kitchen and found a broom leaning against the wall and Chan singing quietly to herself while wiping down the counters with something that smelled lemony.

Her thick blonde hair tumbled down her back, ending before it reached her ass. The new jeans she wore hugged her like a second skin, showing off her enticing curves and slender legs. Josh moved in quietly behind her, trying to decide if he should peel her new clothes off her and fuck her against the counter, pull her over to the table and take her there, or actually throw her over his shoulder and move to the bedroom.

"There's no food here." She turned before he reached her and then leaned against the counter, looking up at him as she slowly licked her lips.

"I see plenty to feast on right in front of me," he growled, clearing the distance between them quickly and pinning her against the counter.

She dropped her cloth and ran damp hands up his chest. The cold from the outside drained out of him and heat hardened every inch as he grabbed her hair and yanked her head back so he could devour her mouth and neck. He loved the new sweater she wore, one he'd picked out and approved of instantly when she tried it on. It was a low-cut V-neck and the lace bra underneath matched the thong she also wore.

Her cleavage swelled and he kept himself from getting too close so he could enjoy the view.

"I'm surprised you have the energy." She rubbed his shoulders, digging her fingers into muscles that screamed with pleasure as she massaged. "I thought I'd go find us supper since you let me sleep all the way here. I bet that lake is full of some awesome fish."

"You aren't going hunting or fishing by yourself." He didn't smile when her classic defiant expression appeared instantly. "Until we know exactly why that asshole wants you so desperately, I'm not letting you out of my sight. That's final."

Chan closed her eyes, exhaling. "I'm accustomed to taking care of myself, and I do it very well. Now I can't even show you gratitude for offering protection by doing some of the work around here. I really don't like this."

It was on the tip of his tongue to tell her he wanted to be more than just her protector. He was her lover, and acknowledging that alone created a warm swelling inside him that grew stronger the longer he stared at her.

She puckered her lips into that sultry, pouty expression of hers, and in spite of her petite size, Chan was anything but defenseless. The coyote attack had done a number on her pride, but he understood and saw her strength, her willingness to take on the unknown and fight for what she believed was right.

"Chan, open your eyes," he said, moving his fingers through her hair and then stroking her face and neck.

She blinked, looking up at him. His scent filled the air and he knew it came from her as well as him.

"You know I'm more than—" He didn't finish his sentence.

A pounding on the door kept him from telling her how much she was starting to mean to him. He turned, the protector she claimed him to be coming forth with so much strength that he growled as he glared at the doorway leading into the living room.

"Who knows we're here?" Chan asked quietly, softly stroking his back with her fingers.

Her touch fueled the urge to protect. In spite of her courageous nature, her fiery personality and willingness to attack and defend without hesitation, Chan was a petite and gorgeous female. His mark was on her, his scent embedded in her flesh, and that wasn't something he took lightly. Maybe other males might come inside a female and then leave. Not Josh. This was a first for him, and it meant something because she meant something. Even if he willingly broke off the sentence, uncertain still of the exact words to describe the building tension inside him that demanded he care for her, he wouldn't deny its existence.

"Open the fucking door," a male howled, pounding louder.

Chan shrieked, digging her nails into his back. The pinching pain caused his muscles to harden and he put out his arm, keeping her behind him as he moved through the cabin.

"God damn it, Josh. Put her clothes back on her and let us in." The voice was suddenly familiar, the taunting baritone followed by laughter.

"Who is it?" Chan's tone changed as well as her scent.

Josh unlocked the front door and pulled it open. His cousin Thad grinned mischievously and tried looking past him.

"Where is she?" he asked. "I can smell her. You going to let us in?"

Josh didn't move but stared at the male standing next to his cousin.

Thad straightened and turned to the male next to him who studied Josh with a serious expression.

"Joshua Bard, you know Richard Ogden."

The male didn't smell of any hostilities and nodded at Josh. "Everyone calls me Race."

"Why's that?" Josh still didn't move, taking his time sizing up this new male.

Race shrugged, his thick knit sweater making his shoulders and chest look broader than they probably were. "When I was a cub I always wanted to race everyone. The nickname stuck."

"I always wondered about that," he mused. "Where are you from?" Josh continued with his interrogation, breathing in the male's scent and searching for any sign of discrepancy that would make him question the other's sincerity for being here, which Josh assumed was to help plot against Leo Pard. But he would learn the male's motives soon enough.

"Actually, my litter is down in Minneapolis. Thad and I have done a fair amount of communicating since all of this bullshit started and I came up here after finding all the leopards I was asked to round up for old Leo. I found them, dropped them off at Birdie's, collected my payment for services rendered and then severed communication." Race glanced over at Thad and then turned, reaching for a box that sat on the ground behind him. He lifted it easily although it appeared to be filled with beer. The rich aroma of fresh meat dominated all other smells quickly though. "I'd be surprised if you weren't cautious of anyone coming around you. Strange shit is going on right now and we all need to be watchful. Your cousin and I thought you two probably haven't had time to do any hunting. We come with fresh meat and beer."

"Good bribes." Josh breathed in the rich smell of the steaks as Race carried the box inside.

Chan tried darting around Josh, eager to play hostess and take the food to the kitchen.

"Let the male carry it," he grumbled, putting his hand on her shoulder and giving her a look he hoped she understood.

"Fine. And I'll prepare it." She smiled broadly then bound into the kitchen after the other two males.

Josh wanted to leap on her and yank her back to his side.

"It's already cooked." Chan clapped her hands together, her happiness drowning out the smell of the meat.

Thad and Race beamed, obviously affected by her enthusiasm. Josh fought not to send both of them tumbling out the back door.

"Food is usually a good way to earn respect," Race offered, and winked at her.

Chan's humble smile was enough to torture any male to his knees.

Josh growled, unable to keep the fierce emotions churning inside him at bay any longer. Thad and Race looked at him. Josh moved in front of Chan. "And it's appreciated. We just got here and haven't had time to hunt yet."

Race's expression turned serious, as did Thad's.

"Which is why we brought it over," Thad said. "The owls told us you'd arrived, although I'm sure you guessed that. They said they followed as you drove here."

"Yeah, I saw them." When Josh turned to the living room, the males showed they had some respect and took his lead.

They walked into the room and Josh sat down, willing to let Chan do what seemed to make her happy, and that was to serve them. Thad and Race made small talk, discussing everything from sports to the weather until they got down to leopard politics.

Chan glowed when she walked in with three plates, balancing them as if she'd been waiting tables all her life. "This food looks great," she said, beaming, and then hurrying back to the kitchen for her plate and four beers.

Josh jumped up to help her and passed out the bottles then sat on the couch next to her. The males sat in chairs facing them and picked up the conversation.

"There is a bit of information that Race sniffed out earlier today." Thad dug into his steak and glanced over at the other male.

"Yeah, it's rather interesting." Race glanced at Chan but then focused on his food. "It appears this male who calls himself Leo Pard wants Chantelle." He nodded at Chan but then looked at Josh. "I mean Chan. Somehow he's got test results that show she can see things stronger than any other leopard. But there's more. He also claims these tests confirm she's part of his litter."

"Test results." Chan coughed and quickly gulped her beer. "What test results?"

She looked at Josh, frowning as all color faded from her face, and then focused on the other two. The spicy smell of her anger flooded the room.

"Trust me. I know who my litter is and he isn't part of it," she hissed, her look turning venomous. "Why would he claim to have test results?"

"Have you seen a doctor recently?" Thad asked.

"Of course not." She gave him a look as if he were crazy. Leopards seldom saw doctors unless they were injured so severely their own metabolism couldn't heal them. "What kind of doctor, and what kind of test would determine if I saw images?"

"That's what I was just thinking," Josh said, finishing off his steak and reaching for his beer. "What is it exactly that you heard? And how did you hear it?"

Race finished off his beer and placed the empty bottle on the coffee table. He sat in a rocking chair near the fire and picked up the poker, doing the honors of pushing the logs around to get the fire going again.

"Earlier today," Race began, and then looked at Thad.

Thad scrubbed his short dark blond hair and looked worried when he met Josh's gaze. "I'm not into chasing my tail or anything, so I'm not going to swear to any of this shit. But we're worried that possibly when she was taken by the coyotes they might have done something to her."

"Done something to her?" Josh growled, pulling his glare from his cousin to Chan.

She looked at Thad wide-eyed, holding her beer in midair. "What exactly do you mean?" she whispered.

Josh put his beer on the coffee table and wrapped his arm around Chan. She stiffened slightly but didn't stop him from pulling her next to him. He looked over her head from Thad to Race.

"Exactly what are you saying?" he demanded.

154

Race scowled at the coffee table, speaking slowly and with a serious edge that stilled the room. "When I spoke to Tore earlier, he suggested there were blood tests taken recently that confirmed that Chantelle Drap is Leo Pard's cub. He claims he's her sire."

Chapter Eleven

🔊

The small cabin became really warm. After hand-washing the plates Chan had found in the cabinet and putting everything away, she needed fresh air. The back door off the kitchen was stuck at first, but she made sure it was unlocked and then pulled until it squeaked open. The screen door had some seriously rusty hinges. No one would sneak in or out of this door.

Josh would pounce on her any minute, which had its moments of being exciting. She stepped outside, instantly seeing her breath, and then leaned against the rough wood exterior. Crossing her arms against the biting cold air, she stared at the inky-black sky with millions of stars that almost blinded her.

"Thad and Race just left." Josh appeared in the doorway, standing just inside the screen door. "They'll be back in the morning."

"Hmm," she grunted, smelling Josh's strong male scent that her body instantly responded to. Too much was hitting her at once. With every breath, whether he was around her or not, she breathed in Josh. It was such a wonderful smell and made her feel good, comfortable, at peace and protected. But she didn't want a male wrapped around her so tight she couldn't breathe, couldn't move without him tugging on some damned leash.

"Are you okay?" His soft baritone soothed her senses.

"I don't know." She hated the urge that rushed through her to turn around, pull open the screen door and fall into his arms. "If you sired someone, would you allow them to be attacked and then let them go?"

"If I had a cub and believed they sincerely wanted to be with someone they cared about instead of me, then I might let them go." He spoke slowly, sounding as if he chose his words carefully. "And we don't have any proof he had anything to do with the coyotes attacking you. We know he paid them, but possibly he paid for your return after learning you were there. I won't pass judgment without all the facts."

"Good grief!" Chan pushed away from the wall and marched into the yard, throwing her arms up in the air and glaring at the panoramic view of so many large stars above her. "Leo Pard is not my sire!"

"I believe you." Josh pushed the screen door open and let it bang shut. "Where is your sire?"

She didn't turn around. Instead, lowering her head, she hugged herself and watched her breath form a foggy cloud in front of her face. "They're both dead," she said simply, remembering all too well the chilly night, the star-filled sky, and the onslaught of emotions that tumbled through her the evening that changed her life.

"My parents are dead too." He didn't say it as if he wanted sympathy.

Josh remained a few feet behind her, far enough that she didn't feel his body heat. He could be a mile away and she would still smell him, but it seemed he understood she didn't want sympathy. He read her too easily, and she searched inside herself for irritation that he seemed to know her so well. She couldn't find it. Just the same, she ached for him to comfort her, to hold her and make all the odd feelings go away. Yet he was the reason for them. And if he did comfort her, he might capture her heart.

"I don't get why he would say he's my sire." Keeping the subject on something she could be pissed about was safer territory. Hard, angry emotions kept her grounded. The last thing she could allow right now were feelings that would trip her, fog her senses and prevent her from smelling how things really were. "If he went to the trouble to seek me out, then you'd think he would have sniffed after me for a while. It wouldn't take much to learn I'm a normal female leopard."

"How many females do you know?"

She spun around, slapping her hair from her face, and frowned at his calm expression. "What kind of question is that?"

Josh smiled gently, his green eyes and blond-red curls reflecting the glow from all of the stars and the moon above them. "I've never met another female like you."

Chan shook her head. She didn't want romance, or that soft, affectionate look Josh kept giving her. It was bad enough fighting the urge to clear the distance between them. Her body screamed for his touch. Swelling grew inside just from him staring at her. They'd only known each other a few days and she shouldn't feel anything more for him other than physical desire.

"That's not what I meant." She ignored his implication. "You have visions. Hell, according to what you've told me, there are twenty leopards who were sought out because they could see things others can't. I don't see anything that makes sense half of the time. There's nothing about me that makes me any better than anyone else on that list."

"Maybe there is." He walked toward her. "How did your parents die?"

"What does that have to do with anything?" She marched away from him, the cold air sinking deeper into her flesh. Her body grew pinched with the need to change, to harden her flesh and fend off the chill that made her shake and her knees wobble.

Josh's hand gripped her shoulder, his body heat singing her skin. "When I was a cub, our litter was on a nightly run. My parents were attacked and killed." She closed her eyes, refusing to let the memory surface. If only she'd seen those leopards coming. They jumped on her parents so quickly there wasn't anything she could do to help. Her littermates tried to save her sire and mother. Two of them died for their efforts. Today it was just her and Charles.

"That really sucks. I'm sorry," she said, hugging herself and turning toward the cabin. She either needed to get back into the warmth, or change and run until she couldn't run any farther. As much as the latter sounded damned appealing, right now she just wanted to be alone.

Josh was right on her heels though and spun her around when they were in the kitchen. "Chan, did your parents die the same way? Were they attacked when you were a cub?"

"What's it matter if they were?" She trembled uncontrollably. "We're aggressive hunters. Many of us die while fighting in our fur." She gathered her hair behind her head and blew out a breath. "I really don't want to talk about it, Josh. It's not a pleasant memory."

"It's probably the worst memory there is," he whispered, and gripped her shoulders. "Chan, we are killers. Leopards fight and many of us die. But our parents were ambushed while we were cubs, and if I'm right, both of our parents died by leopards we didn't know. And those leopards disappeared right afterward. None of the litters we knew had a clue who they were." He moved his hand, sending chills rushing over her flesh as his rough fingertips moved under her chin and then forced her head up to look at him. "I don't know about you, Chan, but I would love to avenge my parents' death."

"You're saying you think our parents were killed by the same leopards." Her heart pounded too hard to think. And she needed to think. "That doesn't make sense. Our litter was in Phoenix. I was ten."

"I was also ten." His brooding expression intensified his strong cheekbones. He moved his thumb, slowly rubbing just underneath her jawbone. The slight action ignited sparks inside her that made it impossible to look away from his eyes. They were the source of her heat, the smoldering desire that burned furiously in his gaze and passed to her through his touch, his focused stare. "I think a plot has been put into play that possibly began when we were just cubs."

"What plot is that?" She forced her gaze away from his, focusing on the dark kitchen window, but his touch continued to fog her brain.

"You heard him when he claimed to be my sire. And now he claims to be yours? We both know that isn't possible." He stared over her head, his scent growing strong with irritation. "I'm not sure what is going on yet. But we aren't cubs anymore. And Pard, or anyone else backing him, won't take anything else from us — ever."

She swallowed roughly and almost staggered when she stepped backward. "I need some time, Josh," she said hoarsely.

"Time for what?"

"I don't know. To think. To clear my head." She stared up at him, exasperated that she needed to explain. "I smell you, feel you. Damn it — you've made me need you." She backed up quickly when he stepped closer. "I'll take the bedroom. You can sleep by the fire. I just need to sort all of this out in my head."

"Whatever." He didn't move, although his arms stiffened at his side and his jawline flexed, as if it took incredible effort on his part to not come closer. "You close yourself in that bedroom and you'll freeze."

"Then I'll leave the bedroom door open. We've already established trust, remember?" She turned and hurried away from him, barely able to stand looking at his face when it was etched with so much anger and pain.

* * * * *

Sleeping alone had never bothered Chan before. Possibly because before, when she was alone, she slept. But tossing and turning, tearing at the blankets she'd warmed in the dryer earlier, simply made her grumpy. And her brain was worse for wear come morning.

Padding barefoot across the cold floor into the kitchen, Chan started coffee and then scratched at her tangled mane while staring outside at the sunrise. She probably looked like shit, but didn't care. Maybe it would do Josh some good to see how foul-tempered she was, that in fact she was tainted by nature, rough and damned sure not ready for anything that leaned toward the edge of permanent.

Life just didn't work that way. At least not her life. There were no definites, no solid ground that would always be there. Since she was ten. Charles had done his best, kept them together, but even then, Chan knew heading out on her own allowed him to create his own litter. And it sounded as if he had. She bit her lip, glancing down as the coffee slowly dripped into the pot. Creating a litter, settling down and claiming a small piece of this earth wouldn't be in the script for her. The images she saw never made sense until recently. And even now she couldn't put all the pieces together. But Josh was right about one thing, her life had been fucked up since she was a cub. And she wouldn't bring another litter into this world, only for them to know pain and suffering if they lost their mother or sire. Taking a mate couldn't happen.

But the only way to get Josh's scent off her was to leave and quit thinking about him. One would be damned hard to do, the other near impossible.

The coffeemaker grumbled and the rich coffee smell tickled her nose. She reached for the cabinet to grab a cup. But the cabinet wasn't there. It was cold, too damned cold. And her feet were wet.

"Chan! Change! Change now!" Josh screamed, his voice garbled.

She turned, almost sliding when she realized the grass was covered with dew. Josh wasn't ten feet away from her and already black rosettes covered his muscular body. His mouth moved again, his eyes glowing fiercely. A deadly roar came out instead of words. Chan grabbed her shirt, confused but feeling the change unleash inside her. As she started to pull her sweater over her head, something caught her eye.

Leopards. Several of them. For a moment she was confused. She saw the leopards bound out of the trees, just as they had when she was a cub. They leapt, teeth bared, claws unsheathed, muscles rippling under their thick hides.

They weren't cubs anymore.

This would not fucking happen twice!

No! she screamed.

Chan slapped the counter so hard the coffeemaker jumped and the pot rattled against the plastic. Something banged in the other room and she shrieked. When she turned, she realized she'd started undressing and changing in the kitchen.

"God. Crap." Her words were mumbled growls.

She sucked in deep breaths, beyond humiliated and pissed an image hit her that hard. She dropped her head and pressed her palm to her forehead.

"Fuck," she hissed, proud the one word came out so clear.

"God damn, Chan." Josh's body was warm, and in spite of so much muscle he was cuddly. His arms went around her, not asking, but pulling her against him. "What the hell happened?"

"I saw something." She relaxed against him. Later she would deploy her strategies to keep him at a distance. Right now Josh felt too damned good to let him go. "I thought I was outside and my feet were wet."

"I take it that's not what made you scream." He had the good sense not to sound humored, but instead held her firm against his chest with one arm. He opened the cabinet, pulled out another cup and poured coffee for both of them. "Come with me. Tell me what just happened."

Chan accepted the cup, instantly feeling the warmth seep through the ceramic. She followed Josh into the living room, noticing for the first time that he was naked. She focused on his hard ass and then shot her gaze up his broad back then down his long, muscular legs. Dark hair covered tanned skin. Corded, roped muscles flexed as he moved like a deadly predator, silent and steady.

When he stepped around the coffee table, he turned to face her and then leaned over to pull the blanket off the floor where it probably tumbled when she startled him awake.

"Sit," he ordered, making room on the couch and then setting his cup on the coffee table.

All she wore was the simple cotton nightgown she'd purchased the day before. Although Josh looked at her with mild disgust when she'd selected it, Chan wasn't going to prance around someone else's home naked when it was bedtime. But now the spaghetti straps didn't want to stay on her shoulders and the thin material rubbed over her nipples, making them extra sensitive. She stepped around the coffee table and sat on the couch, instantly feeling enveloped by Josh's warmth and strong, overwhelming scent. She felt the indention from where he'd slept. Even though he sat next to her, not touching her, it was as if he were wrapped around her, drowning her with his body heat and incredibly intoxicating and appealing aroma.

"What did you see?"

She sipped her coffee and stared at the glowing embers in the fireplace. "Well," she started, hating this part about her images the most. They were usually flashes in her brain, like dreams, and repeating them out loud made her sound ridiculous. "I was outside," she added, nodding toward the kitchen and then frowning.

"Go on," he prompted, leaning sideways into the couch and facing her.

She glanced at him and then drank more coffee. His naked body sprawled out next to her didn't help in retaining the details of what she'd seen. Even relaxed his cock looked thick. Her insides swelled with need so quickly she couldn't remember her name let alone the images she just saw.

"Okay," she said, blowing out a puff of air and turning so she sat on the edge of the couch. The fabric held his heat from where he'd slept and crept over her like a very warm blanket. She jumped up, hopping around the coffee table and then started pacing. "I was outside."

"You said that already."

"I know."

"Why did you scream?"

"I wanted to warn you."

"That you were having a vision?" He tilted his head, studying her but maintaining a serious expression.

Which was a damned good thing. If he even started to crack a smile over her difficulties in focusing, she would pounce with all claws extended.

"No," she snapped, and stopped pacing.

"I know. They're hard to describe after they happen. Just take your time." His soothing tone was about as much help as his enticing scent.

Chan closed her eyes, pressing her palm to her forehead and tried replaying the images she saw over in her mind. "I went into the kitchen to make coffee. I didn't sleep well and so just stood there staring out the window while it brewed. Then I was outside and you were yelling at me. When I saw the leopards leap at you, it reminded me of when they attacked my parents. And I can't handle losing someone else who..."

She broke off. Then quickly added when she remembered. "You yelled at me to change. You screamed that I needed to change."

She didn't realize her eyes were moist until she blinked, which released the salty smell into her hand. God. She might as well march right back into that bedroom and start this day over. As if she wanted anyone smelling her humiliation.

"Chan."

"What," she snapped.

"Come here."

"God. Why?" She dropped her hand, refusing to wipe her eyes, and glared at him.

"Come here, Chan."

His brooding expression darkened while he watched her. She wasn't sure her legs would carry her. Simply staring at him, naked, half reclined against the corner of the couch, his long legs taking up more than half of the leg room space. She never would have guessed anyone could look so dangerous naked, in their flesh, while vegged-out on a couch.

"I'm fine," she grumbled, downing the rest of her coffee and then ignoring his command, doing an about-face toward the kitchen. She refilled her cup and when he didn't follow her, she slowly moped back to him.

"Come here," he repeated. He hadn't moved a muscle when she left for more coffee. "I know you're fine."

"Liar," she grumbled, determined she wouldn't feel sorry for herself. She marched over to the couch and sat on the opposite end from Josh.

He moved faster than she anticipated, grabbed her, took her cup and placed it on the coffee table then dragged her over his body as he reclined once again in his corner. "I'm not lying," he grumbled. "You're very fine."

She stared at her fingers, which were stretched over his heart. The strong steady pulse throbbed through her. Along with his body heat, which simmered everywhere he touched her, his hard-packed body pressed against hers was too much to handle.

"I make you sleep on the couch and now you're being nice to me."

"I'm one hell of a leopard," he growled, his baritone vibrating through his chest.

165

"Yeah you are." She didn't stop him when he lifted her nightgown and then pulled it free from her body. Experience taught her if she hesitated a bit, he'd probably shred the nightgown, and she kind of liked this one.

Josh tossed her gown to the floor and placed his finger under her chin, tilting her head. Chan couldn't take it anymore. She climbed up his body like a cat would a tree. Josh tried grabbing her wrist. She slapped it.

"Behave," she growled.

He raised one eyebrow. She wasn't sure if she saw disbelief or amusement. Either way he obeyed. And his scent intoxicated her. She nipped at his neck, tasting and smelling him at the same time. When he grabbed her ass and stretched her open, the sudden sensation of being vulnerable, exposed, made her want to be even more aggressive.

Her vision disturbed her. She'd never seen anything that didn't happen eventually, although she never knew if what she saw would happen in five minutes or five months. But this one smelled bad, really bad, and until she understood it, had time to figure out what she saw, she needed to clear her head. Demanding Josh submit to her sounded better than a hard, long run.

She pushed on his shoulders, lifting herself over him and pressed her breasts into his face. He squeezed her ass, kneading it and dragging his fingers closer to her heat.

Josh clamped down on one of her nipples, nipping and sucking eagerly when she brushed her breast across his face. She tilted her head back, closing her eyes and arching into him. Bending her arms and pressing her hands into his shoulders, she straddled him and found his hard, eager cock ready to give her what she needed.

It was her turn not to ask. Her turn to take control and say how things would be. For once in her life she would leap and take pleasure for herself without worrying about the consequences or what anyone might think.

"Don't move," she instructed, and pushed away from him.

He raised his lids lazily and looked at her with an incredibly dangerous gaze. Something flickered in his gaze, as if the thought of being submissive, even if it required simply doing nothing, took more than just a bit of effort on Josh's part.

She smiled at his silent, challenging expression and raised her body so his cock could bounce to life underneath her. She lowered herself on it, pushed down.

She hissed. It wasn't even a human sound. His cock glided inside her, stretching and filling her, building a pressure that peaked so quickly and then exploded. It was all she could do not to fall forward. He hit that spot, breaking the dam and sending wave after wave of pleasure ripping through her.

"No," she managed to say. And when she moved to grab his wrists, he shifted inside her, brushing against muscles that were so tender, so sensitive to his touch, that she almost leapt off him.

Somehow she dug her nails into his flesh, almost puncturing his skin, and held on.

"You don't like this?" His words were raspy.

"No." She shook her head adamantly, sending her hair flying over her face. "Let go."

His chuckle helped build her determination and clear her head just a bit from the sexual fog that clogged her ability to think straight. Opening her eyes, she narrowed them on him, hissing out a breath, and then used all the force she could muster to move his hands from her ass.

When he cooperated and lifted his arms, she almost fell forward and pinned his hands over his head.

"Behave," she growled, her face inches above his and her hair creating an intimate shroud that narrowed their world down to the two of them.

"I always behave." He thrust his hips upward, impaling her with his cock.

"Oh God!" She was at the definite disadvantage. "Crap," she said through clenched teeth while she struggled to lift herself off him.

Josh reclined on the couch, half slumped with his head leaning in the corner and his hands relaxed over his head. His legs took up most of the space and she straddled him with one leg propped up leaning against the back of the couch and the other on the floor. She steadied herself, half standing, and pressed his wrists together, feeling him throb while his cock seemed to swell inside her.

He was just so much bigger than she was and seemed perfectly content to let her struggle for control while he lay there, completely relaxed other than his rock-hard cock. The more she fought to ride him, to determine when she would come again, the more he grew inside her. Chan felt the pressure build, her orgasm teetering so close to the edge she could hardly breathe.

She wanted to say when they came, and she wanted them to come together. As fucking huge as he was, he had to be on the brink of explosion.

She opened her eyes, her hair draping down around his head. He stared up at her with eyes that glowed a magnificent emerald green. When his lips parted, she fought the urge not to lower her mouth to his. But she'd found her rhythm, moving up and down, creating a slow, soothing, sensation as his cock stroked her pussy and built her up to a climax she could enjoy. Not one that was ripped out of her, leaving her breathless and unable to function.

Control. That's what she needed. Sex was best when she could enjoy every wonderful sensation. And Josh's cock rubbed her soaked muscles, soothed the ache and craving that made her more and more frustrated throughout the night. As the tension slowly oozed out of her, the pressure and need to come filled her with so much intensity she swore her world tilted to the side.

Suddenly all of her senses were heightened. Every breath she took was rich and clean, smelling like the two of them. No longer did each of them have their own scent, but a new, erotic aroma swelled around her. She heard every breath she took, raspy and needy. And Josh, breathing steady and deep. They inhaled and exhaled together, sharing the air that was perfumed with their united scent. His face seemed to glow, even in the shadows created from her hair falling forward around them.

Chan stared at his parted lips and lifted herself, feeling him ease out of her and then bringing him back deep inside her, sucking every inch of him deep into her womb.

"Chan." His lips barely moved.

She saw the strain in his expression. She ached to run her tongue over his flesh, taste him in her mouth. He moved his tongue, barely licking his lips, and then breathed in just when she did.

"Come," she demanded.

He twitched again inside her and a shiver rushed over her.

"Come with me," he growled.

"Okay."

He thrust up hard, and then again.

"Wait!" she tried saying, but her howl only fueled his fervor.

He thrust harder, impaling her clear up to her bellybutton. She toppled forward and his hands came up, lifting hers along with his.

Chan growled, her teeth growing and piercing her lip. The metallic taste of blood gave her newfound strength and she leapt off him, jumping backward and almost falling over the coffee table. She managed to leap over it, but Josh flew through the air like a giant predator, his curls twisting around his face while his eyes glowed with power and strength she couldn't conquer.

But damn him if he wouldn't obey.

"Down now," she screamed.

He stopped, momentarily looking confused.

Chan pointed to the floor. "Lie down on the floor now, leopard. Or I swear you'll be jacking off in the shower."

He growled, taking a step toward her, his own energy on overload and muscles twitching all over his body.

"Don't tell me what to do," he growled.

"Damn straight I will, and you'll listen." She shook when she pointed to the floor, one finger extended while her nails cut into her palm. Every inch of her shook, her insides empty and needing his cock back so badly she could barely stand. "Lie down on the floor," she said, speaking each word slowly while even her lips shook.

He was so much taller than she was, and she looked up at his face, continuing to point while staring him down. Her skin itched, tingled with more energy than her human body could handle. She wouldn't look away though, wouldn't pull her gaze from his.

Gold flickered in his green eyes when he slowly moved. Josh didn't look away either when he knelt, moved to stretch out on the floor. She didn't hesitate but quickly straddled him, her muscles quivering so badly she worried she'd make an ass out of herself and change.

Her legs were barely long enough to straddle him and have her knees touch the ground. So propping herself up to a squatting position, she stroked his cock with her soaked entrance, purring.

She blinked, looking at him, surprised to hear the sincere sound of pleasure emerge from her throat. He didn't smile, didn't mock her with his amused expression, but looked at her so seriously that a wash of emotions attacked her too hard to breathe.

Chan moved just enough to pull his cock upward and then easily slid down on it.

"God, yes," she breathed, licking her lips and closing her eyes as pure bliss washed over her.

"Open your eyes." He spoke so gently, reaching for her face, softly stroking her hair behind her shoulder.

Chan blinked, increasing speed without thinking about it as she started fucking him with all the energy stored inside her. She opened her eyes and then quickly sucked in a breath as she watched the beautiful streaks of gold highlight his green eyes.

"I love you," he whispered, and then his facial muscles tightened.

She couldn't speak, couldn't comment, and sure as hell couldn't look away. Her insides exploded and an array of bright light washed over her line of vision. She arched over him, pressing her fingers into his rock-hard chest.

Josh grabbed her hips and thrust. Once. Twice. A growl ripped from him loud enough to shake the cabin. He filled her with so much heat as he came she swore she felt his love fill every inch of her.

Chapter Twelve

Thad and Race were there again. This time when they showed up, they brought a couple of owls with them.

"No offense against your species," Dover said, his soft-spoken manner typical of his kind. "Far be it for me to spook a panthera."

"Piss me off and you'll be more than spooked." After a few beers Chan finally joined in on the conversation. Her easy smile showed she challenged more than warned Dover.

"All I meant was that word is traveling fast and an uneasy leopard isn't always a friendly leopard." Dover lifted his bottle of beer in a silent salute to Chan and then drank.

"The problem is there's no common ground among us," Josh said, watching the condensation drip down the outside of his bottle. "Leo Pard is making waves, but none of us know where to go, or who to turn to, whom they can trust."

"I trust everyone in this room," Race offered. "But outside of these walls, I wouldn't trust anyone with my tail."

Josh would say the same. He looked over at Chan, who focused on her bottle and meticulously removing the label. Ever since their lovemaking, she'd been quiet. Her aggressiveness turned him on more than he ever guessed it would. Telling her he loved her wasn't intentional. But now that he'd said it, he didn't regret it. The only thing that bothered him was her unusual silence ever since then. The scent that came off both of them while they were fucking was too strong not to notice. They were bonding—mating. And that couldn't be reversed.

She glanced up at him and he held her gaze for a moment, seeing her eyes cloud with worry. Standing, he watched her eyes widen when he walked across the living room to stand next to where she sat in the rocking chair.

"It's crossed my mind to create a place where leopards can come and know they are safe." Everyone looked at him when he spoke. "We don't run in packs, and until we mate, most often we run alone. But Leo is creating a situation that will change how we live. He is trying to pull leopards together he feels are the best of our kind. If we're going to fight him, we need some form of unification."

"Where would this place be?" Thad asked.

"You've been to Birdie's." Tyton, another owl, sat at one of the kitchen table chairs he'd dragged into the living room. He sat with the chair backward and his long legs straddling it. "He offers sanctuary to any species but this place isn't large enough."

"There's plenty of land and we own it. It might be worth adding on." Josh caught Thad's interest. "There's leopards in the area who might help."

"Leopards aren't the only ones who can build." Dover stood with his empty bottle and headed toward the kitchen.

Chan looked toward the window at the same time Josh heard something crackle outside. Everyone in the room tensed. He put his hand protectively on Chan's shoulder but she stood quickly. She sniffed the air and looked toward the kitchen.

"Stay here." He squeezed her shoulder and then pushed her gently back into the rocking chair. "I mean it."

She jumped back up, almost falling into his chest. "But my vision," she whispered.

The other males were already opening the front door and moving around the cabin. She was his problem, and they would leave him to do what he wanted with her.

"Which is exactly why I want you to stay put." Every vision he ever had came true sooner or later. There had never been an exception. "It's not going to happen the way you saw it."

"But..."

He grabbed her shoulders and pulled her up to him, kissing her savagely. Then he pushed her back into the rocking chair, her taste on his lips and in his mouth. God he wanted more of her already.

"Stay put. I'll be right back." For once he prayed she would listen, understand how real these fucking visions were that they both kept having. If she kept her tail put, and didn't come sniffing after him, maybe, just fucking maybe, they could break the odds.

He headed outside, already doubting his cute little female would listen to him and decided he would do a quick run around the cabin and then get back inside to her. He didn't see what she saw, and wasn't sure if the ramifications of it were good or bad. But it terrified her enough that she almost changed into a leopard in the kitchen, which was something no one did pretty much after the age of four or so.

He headed around the corner of the building when something crashed in the trees next to the cabin. Every inch of him hardened to stone. His teeth and claws extended as his spine prickled. The urge to change had never hit him so hard. Josh glared at the trees and then about turned and sprung at the person who ran around the house behind him.

"There are leopards." It was amazing how owls sounded calm even when their actions showed how tense they were.

Josh studied Dover's large dark eyes that didn't blink but watched him and then the grounds around them intently. "Where? How many?"

"At least several. And they are coming from the highway on foot and in their fur."

He glanced toward the area of woods where he'd just heard the crashing sound and then headed that direction. "Take a look overhead and see what you find," he said over his shoulder.

"Tyton is already flying around." Dover's shoulders began expanding as he spoke. "I'll head up there with him and warn you if there's serious trouble."

Josh barely glanced over his shoulder as the owl stripped out of his clothes and started transforming. He didn't doubt for a moment there was trouble. Maybe he should have forced Chan to give every detail of her vision to him instead of allowing her to calm down and make love to him. Although who the hell was he fooling, he wanted her so desperately that he hadn't slept at all during the night. All he did was lie there and breathe in her scent while listening to her breathing in the other room. He should have fucking guessed a vision that would terrify her to that extent meant serious trouble was right around the corner.

Or in this case, right around the trees. He smelled it before he entered the thick line of forest alongside the cabin.

The leopard looked at him and roared, his teeth and fur covered with sticky dark red blood. The corpse underneath him must have just died. Slowly it changed back to its human form.

"What the fuck?" Josh growled, ignoring Thad's possessive growl and glancing through the trees and then back at the cabin. "I bet you find his meat a bit tough. See who else is around here and don't let anyone near the cabin."

Thad roared again but then leapt over the dead male who now lay naked in his full human form. Josh took a good look at the face. He didn't know the male and now never would.

Thad raced away through the trees, barely making a sound. Josh was surprised he didn't ache to tear across the land with his cousin. The only thing that mattered though was protecting Chan, and she wasn't in the woods.

The fresh smell of blood drew forth the carnal side of his nature. Even in human form, his predatory side dominated, eager to kill, destroy anyone who would dare enter his domain and fuck with what was his. And although he didn't have a shred of proof, his gut told him why these strangers were here.

Chan.

He was back in the yard alongside the cabin within seconds. Sniffing the air, he picked up the smell of leopards. It was strong. Too strong to be one male or two. Fortunately, he didn't smell any females. He would dwell on why she'd listened to him later. Right now he was just damned glad his little female kept her ass inside.

Someone walked through the backyard and Josh hurried to the end of the cabin. His skin prickled with the urge to attack and he fought to hold on to his human form when Race hurried toward him.

The male stifled a growl, obviously as gunned up as he was. "There were two males up front," he said, his voice gravelly. Race's shirt was untucked and he was barefoot. "I smell more of them but I don't see them. What the fuck is going on?"

"We're being attacked." He glanced toward the back door. In her vision, Chan told him she came out the back door. Moving closer to it, he would be damned sure to block it if she even tried opening it. "Head around to the other side and roar if you see or hear anything."

Race nodded. "Do the same," he said, turning and running back around the yard to the other side of the cabin.

Josh turned, searching the trees. They were out there. He smelled them, felt them watching him. His skin crawled. His muscles twitched. Every inch of him grew so hard he could barely move. The effort to stay human grew impossible.

Yanking off his shirt, he continued watching the trees, glancing toward the side of the cabin and then around back as he shed his clothes.

He kicked off his second shoe when something snapped before him. Josh would fucking destroy his God damn jeans without hesitating if he had to. If some coward-ass leopard thought he could jump Josh before he finished undressing, they would learn quickly a few things about his nature. One being he didn't give a rat's ass about new clothes. And two being that unexpected company really pissed him off.

His muscles began shifting in his body and he growled fiercely at his surroundings. No one was there. But they were close, hiding—the fucking cowardly bastards.

"You think sneaking up on me is going to give you a fighting chance?" he yelled at the trees. "Bring it on, motherfuckers. You are going to die either way. Let's get it over with and maybe I'll be merciful. But don't count on it," he added under his breath.

He unzipped his jeans and swore the branches rustled more than a breeze would cause. Blood pumped through his veins, building speed as pain ripped down his spine. He welcomed the pain, the incredible strength it brought, the freedom from human emotions and hesitation. It was all cut and dried in his fur. Protect, conquer and maintain. Pretty fucking simple.

Someone growled. So they wanted to play. Josh sniffed the air, easily grabbing the scents of at least two males in their fur. They were waiting—waiting for him to change. Then the oddest thought hit him. No one else had had a vision over what was about to happen, did they?

A roar from the other side of the cabin caused him to rip his jeans with his claws. "Shit," he hissed, suddenly pissed at how close he just came to doing himself some serious damage.

His anger didn't subside when more screams sounded from toward the front of the house. He turned, ready to rip out of his jeans. Race was up there and it didn't sound good. Something moved among the trees. He glanced in that direction and saw a leopard before it disappeared behind foliage.

Ambush.

The back door opened.

177

God damn it. No. It was her fucking vision. Didn't she know it would be bad?

Chan stepped outside, glancing down at the ground and her bare feet. When she looked up, fear mixed with confusion in her torn expression.

"Change," he hissed at her. Already his body was making speech difficult. But his little female was going to disobey him. And she'd be a hell of a lot safer in her fur right now than in her skin. "Change now!"

"No!" she screamed as she yanked off her shirt.

Her gaze was pinned behind him. Josh spun around, giving up on his jeans and letting the change consume him. The denim tore from his body and he fell to all fours. But he didn't stay there. Leaping into the air, he took on the three leopards like a bowling ball attacking pins. They all went toppling in different directions.

Josh dug his claws into the ground, feeling the earth seep between the pads of his paws as he forced himself to a stop. The angry high-pitched growl behind him didn't reassure him. Fighting off these bastards would be a hell of a lot easier if he didn't have to protect Chan while doing it.

He turned quickly and then anger turned to blind rage when four more leopards raced around from the side of the house and leapt onto Chan.

She screamed, the terror and shock in her eyes forcing outrage to pump through him at a dangerous speed. He tore into first one leopard and then the next one, fighting viciously while Chan struggled to keep them off her.

They would die. All of them would fucking die. She was his. And these low-life assholes weren't going to lay a damned paw on her without seriously regretting it.

One of the males he sent flying got up and came at him again. Josh sneered, curling his lip as he stared the bastard in the eyes.

178

You really don't want to fuck with me, he told the creep with a low, cruel growl.

While the jerk decided whether to listen or not, Josh leapt at another leopard who tried pouncing on Chan. He didn't hear the leopard coming from behind him. The screams from the sky were a bit too fucking late. Another leopard pounced on him and then another.

Where the hell were they all coming from?

His world became one of fur, claws and teeth.

Chan! he screamed.

There were too many growls and hisses in his ears to hear if she answered. Claws and teeth sliced at his flesh. He couldn't see anything.

Fucking pricks. Fucking bastards. They would die for this. Every last one of them would regret the day they entered his land. He swore he screamed her name again, but he wasn't sure. Everything around him went black.

* * * * *

"Do you remember any of this?" a deep male voice said.

Chan blinked, feeling sore from her head to her toes. She moved her hand, slowly, and rubbed water from her face. More drops splattered on her cheeks. It hurt like hell to roll over and then slowly push herself to a sitting position. Her hair seemed to be in one large fucking knot.

Where the hell was she?

Everything seemed white for a few moments as she blinked and finally gave up trying to run her fingers through her tangled mess. She stared at the long silver bars surrounding her and the gray sky that spread out endlessly beyond that. Her clothes hung on her all wrong.

"Where am I?" Her voice cracked and no one heard her. She couldn't get her brain to work.

Nothing she saw made sense. Adjusting herself so she sat cross-legged, she looked down around her. Maybe she was dreaming, or worse yet, having another vision. But damn if it didn't look as if she sat in a cage. When she looked up, she swore knives stabbed through her brain. Squeezing her eyes shut, she pressed her palms to her temples.

"Get a grip, damn it," she told herself. At least her voice sounded right this time.

There were voices, males around her. Although she didn't smell them, just heard their voices. Something was seriously wrong with her. She opened her eyes and noticed how dirty her hands were, as if she'd been in a nasty fight and just changed back to her flesh. Dirt and blood was smeared over her palms and the back of her hands and the underneath of her fingernails were filled with black gook.

"God," she groaned, and then focused on the clothes she wore. "These aren't mine."

"I'm not cruel enough to humiliate you by making you travel naked." The man's voice sounded as if it came from above her.

Chan squinted, the grayish-white sky glaring at her as she made out the dark ominous figure standing a few feet from her on the other side of the bars. "Where am I?" she asked.

"Almost home. Then I promise this insane method of traveling will end. I promise I took personal care in dressing you myself when they brought you to me." The male paused, and although he didn't smile, it looked as if his expression softened. "You're finally with me, Chantelle."

"Who are you?" Her sense of smell still wasn't working. Worse yet, when she got her eyes to focus on the male looking down at her, she realized she sat in a large dog crate, caged like a fucking animal. She glanced around. There were other cages, each holding a male or female, most of them still sleeping. Those who weren't seemed at least as disoriented as she was. "What is this?"

"My chosen ones." His voice was as soothing as an owl's. But he wasn't one of the feathered shifters.

She wasn't sure how she knew without being able to smell him, but he was a leopard. And so were the others in the cages surrounding her. She looked past the man, who seemed content simply standing outside her cage and watching her, and spotted a large semi-truck parked alongside a quiet two-lane highway. The cages were in a large yard. She turned her head, still moving slowly to keep the stabbing pain at bay, and spotted a very large brick home a short distance from them. A long winding driveway led to the home.

"Let me out of this cage," she told the man.

He didn't hesitate but reached into his pocket and pulled out a large ring with lots of keys on it. Fingering through them, he singled one out and then squatted in front of her.

"Your senses will return to you soon," he explained, sliding the key into the lock and turning it. He pulled open the door and reached for her. "Until they do, you'll probably feel odd without the possession of all of your senses. You'll also find you can't change out of your human form."

Chan ignored his hand and crawled out, feeling disgusted with how she felt like an animal being set free. Standing proved a bit more of a chore. She despised his touch instantly when he took her arm gently and helped her maintain her balance.

"I wouldn't suggest trying to walk to the house from here." The male snapped his fingers and grabbed the attention of a group of leopards not too far from them. With a quick gesture, one of them hurried to a pickup and jumped in. "But we'll get you inside where you can bathe and then be brought to me a bit more presentable."

A hundred questions rushed through her brain, which made it hurt more. But for some reason she didn't want to talk to this male. She let him guide her to the truck and help her in on the passenger side. The male gave the driver simple instructions to take her to her room and then closed the passenger door. Chan didn't say anything while the male drove up the narrow driveway and parked in front of the house. He left the truck running and came around to open her door for him.

Chan didn't want him touching her either. She managed to get out on her own and followed him inside. Her brain still wouldn't register right. She felt the cool, smooth floor underneath her with her bare feet and she saw the wealth that was on blatant display with the fine furniture and ornate carvings around her. But without her senses working properly, she couldn't smell, could only visually see without really comprehending what was around her, it was hard to make her brain register what she saw.

The strangest thought hit her while she held on to the banister and struggled climbing the stairs to the second floor. Was this what it was like to be human? To view the world around her, but not really be able to see it? If so, no wonder humans existed without really taking advantage of all that was around them.

"In there," the male told her, and let his gaze travel down her.

She didn't answer, didn't look back at him, but entered the room and closed the door behind her. There wasn't a lock on the doorknob or anywhere on the door. So she leaned on it for a few minutes, simply staring at the room in front of her.

Josh.

Shit. Her head hurt so badly that thinking was almost more of a chore than walking. What had happened?

Chan struggled against the pain to retrieve her memory, to remember what happened prior to her waking up in a cage. She could see the rocking chair. She sat in it. Josh glared down at her. Suddenly she felt his hands on her shoulders, his sexy baritone telling her to stay put.

And she understood. Her vision was about to play out. Something terrible would happen. But she didn't know what it would be.

"And I still don't know what happened." She hated being in the dark. Not being able to figure out what was happening around her was a sensation as bad as claustrophobia.

She moved across the room, slowly putting one foot in front of the other. Her fingers brushed over the large quilt that was spread over a double-sized bed in the middle of the room. Chan touched the tall, narrow dresser, ran her fingers over the cool window panes and stroked the smooth curtains hanging on either side.

The endless gray sky outside didn't help her figure out her location. Undeveloped land spread out forever behind the house. At least her brain registered that she stared at a backyard. There wasn't anyone or anything outside. No outbuildings or garages or outdoor furniture or anything. For as fancy of a home as this, little work had been done to the exterior of it. There were no trees, no bushes, which would make it hard as hell for someone to run and not be spotted. Or for someone to approach the home and not be detected. She stared at a mountain range that faded in and out of the hazy horizon. If only she could change, or get her vision to cooperate better, maybe she could identify the range that at the moment almost looked like a mirage.

Turning from the window, she stared at the bedroom and breathed in deep. The smell of cleaning products had never smelled better in her life. Her senses were returning to her. A cool breeze rattled the window panes behind her and the chill rushed over her backside. Chills rushed down and a spark ignited in her spine.

The male told her she wouldn't be able to change while whatever god-awful drug he injected her with remained in her system. But it was obviously wearing off. She stared at her filthy fingers and willed her claws to grow. Nothing happened other than the knife stabbing through her brain again.

"Crap," she hissed, and dropped her hands to her sides.

There were two other doors in the room besides the one that led to the hallway. One proved to be a closet, and the other a private bathroom. It might still be a cage, but it was a hell of a step up from the silver bars that she woke up to. The closet was lined with shelves and one bar for hanging clothes. Nothing hung on the bar, but there were jeans and shirts folded on the shelves. After checking the sizes, she chose clothes that she could put on and then headed for the bathroom.

A hot shower and then changing it over to a bath did wonders, and the cruel knife finally got the hell out of her head. Chan rubbed the thick towel over her body and inspected herself in the full-length mirror on the backside of the closed bathroom door. The soap and shampoo provided left a lavender scent that hung heavily in the fogged bathroom. She breathed in deep, filling her system with the clean smell and glanced down her naked body.

"I sure as hell hope the other guy looks worse," she told her reflection, and then looked down to closer inspect the cuts and bruises all over her body. She looked a hell of a lot worse than she did when the coyotes attacked her. "And these were my own kind. What the hell is happening to us?"

She remembered leaving Josh's cabin and the leopards leaping at her from every direction. Her heart constricted as the memory came into focus. She'd lost sight of Josh amidst the wall of fur, claws and teeth.

"Please be alive," she prayed. "Please be okay."

He'd told her loved her. His words hummed through her mind, creating a mantra she held on to while dressing. Somehow she needed to figure out where she was and then find a way to reach him. Just knowing he probably didn't have a clue where she was made her sick. Worse yet, did they take him too?

God. Was he one of the leopards outside in one of those cages? She'd been so fucking out of it she didn't pay close enough attention to any of them.

"I would have smelled him." No drug would rob her of the ability to sense him if he were near.

Believing Josh wasn't here somehow gave her strength. But where the fuck was here?

The jeans and white T-shirt fit well enough, but without any underwear, she felt exposed, especially with the white shirt making it possible to see her nipples in the proper lighting. She searched the closet again but found only more shirts and jeans that were identical to the ones she wore.

"Someone has a hell of a taste for fashion," she snarled, although she was grateful to at least be out of the clothes that male made a point of telling her he put on her. And her body was clean, free from the scent of any of the leopards who'd touched her.

Now to get the hell out of here. She looked down at her hands again and this time when she willed her claws to appear, her fingernails transformed, pinching sensation shot up her arms as long claws stretched from the end of her fingers.

She jumped at the sound of someone rapping on the bedroom door. Obviously she wasn't back to full capabilities. Chan clasped her hands behind her back, forcing her claws to recede. Her fingers pinched with discomfort as she focused on who spoke quietly outside the door. There was more than one leopard out there. They knocked again, louder.

"It sure as hell isn't locked," she called out.

The door opened and a familiar face smiled at her while amusement and the salty, pungent scent of caution, possibly even fear, filled the room.

"I see you took a shower. Good." Jin Rose nodded her approval and walked into the bedroom. "How are you feeling?"

"Like shit." She immediately decided that announcing the drug was wearing off might not be to her advantage. Chan looked past her at the stocky male leopard who entered behind Jin. "What happened to me?"

Jin turned, not answering immediately, and took a leather strap from the male. He held a few other items that Chan didn't recognize, but she didn't take time to study them. Instead, she focused on Jin when the female approached her.

Chan instinctively took a step backward and growled. On an impulse, she reached behind her for the bed and then sat down, making a show of not having her balance.

"Leo doesn't tolerate leopards who don't obey his orders," Jin said calmly, and then stretched the black leather strap with her hands. "A few of the hunters hired to do their jobs seemed to think that they could outsmart Leo. That really is impossible to do, you know. It was necessary to gather everyone together using extreme methods. I'm sure though, after a few days, you'll understand completely and this won't be necessary any longer."

Chan looked up at Jin, shocked when she realized the leather strap in Jin's hands was a collar. The female brought it to Chan's neck and Chan slid down the side of the bed.

"You're not putting that thing on me," she hissed, hating that if she fought with her full abilities, it would be apparent the drug was no longer in her system. There was nothing worse than appearing weak, especially in front of this female. "I'm not going to fight you. I promise. You can't put a collar on me."

"Leo thought it would be easier on you if I put it on you than one of the males." Jin held the collar in her hands so Chan could stare at it. Her tone softened and there was something unappealing about her scent. Did the female feel sorry for her? "The collar isn't meant to humiliate you. It really serves several purposes. Think of it more as part of your new uniform."

Chan clamped her teeth together so hard they hurt. She focused on the female's waist, detesting her touch when Jin's fingers brushed over Chan's neck and the collar was secured around her neck.

"You have such pretty hair," Jin said softly. "I would kill for such perfect curls."

And Chan wanted to kill her for putting the collar on her. She refused to look up at Jin, or even acknowledge the compliment. Jin obviously detected the anger that filled the room with its dominating spicy smell.

"This works simply really," Jin said, stepping away from the bed and moving toward the door. "The collar has electronic studs in it. It reads your vital statistics and will also help them learn when you're having visions. Honestly, I don't understand a lot about that part, but I'm sure Leo will answer any questions. He wants you to feel free to move anywhere around the house. As you see, there aren't any locks on the doors. The collar allows us to know where you are. There is one downside to it. If you're told to do something and disobey, it also allows us to punish you."

Chan barely had time to look up when a quick charge of electricity racked her body. She jerked, digging into the bedspread with her claws and biting her lip as the intense pain shot through her body and then instantly disappeared.

"Fuck," she snarled, keeping a hold of the bedspread so she wouldn't leap at the female. "Thanks for the demonstration," she said flatly, raising her eyes slowly and hating the hell out of the female, who watched her warily.

Jin fingered a small black box and then hooked it to the wide black belt that hung low on her waist. Her faded blue jeans and snug-fitting black blouse were a change in attire from the leather she wore the last time Chan saw her. But her black straight hair and dark eyeliner surrounding her green eyes gave the impression she didn't want anyone to know what she truly looked like. In effect, Jin wore enough makeup that Chan guessed without it, she would appear a very different female.

Jin also appeared a master at controlling her emotions. Where at times she seemed to regret the tasks she undertook, at other times she seemed indifferent to the fact her actions were so damned dishonorable.

"It's important to understand your punishment so you'll be more inclined to obey," Jin said, not looking Chan in the eye but instead making sure the box was hooked to her belt properly.

If the male weren't standing silently behind Jin, Chan wouldn't hesitate in pouncing on Jin and scratching her eyes out. Just the suggestion that Chan would obey her, or any other male or female here, brought Chan's blood to a quick, hard boil. The fucking bitch!

"There's one more thing," Jin said, using the same calm tone that was growing more and more irritating with every word she spoke. "I personally don't think you're going to give anyone trouble, especially after you truly understand what's going on here, but Leo insists."

She smiled at Chan as if they were the best of friends. Chan managed to keep the sneer off her face, but maintaining a non-responsive expression was getting harder and harder to do the longer the female stood in front of her.

"What's that?" Chan asked, her tone sounding bored. She fought the fury that bit at her insides, knowing if either of them smelled her reaction to what they were doing to her, it would go a lot harder on her.

Jin held up a small silver piece of metal. "Be patient with me. I haven't secured very many of these yet." Again Jin moved into Chan's space, so that their bodies brushed against each other when Jin reached for the collar.

Chan didn't move but shot her gaze to Jin's face. The female's scent changed abruptly as she stared back at Chan and froze. For a moment she didn't smile, but stared into

Chan's eyes. And for that brief second, the smell of fear filled Chan's nostrils. She didn't move, didn't flinch, didn't even blink as she stared hard at the overly made-up female.

Finally Jin smiled, her expression relaxed although the glint in her eye remained wary. "Let me know if I hurt you," she said quietly, and then pressed her cold fingers against Chan's neck as she messed with the collar. Finally she backed up, staring at Chan's neck and looking very pleased with herself. "There. That's all. The snap ensures you can't remove the collar. Although like I said, I bet you don't have to wear it for too long." Jin turned to the door and followed the male to the hallway. "Someone will come get you soon."

Chan stared at the closed door after Jin and the male left her alone. This time she clearly heard their footsteps as they walked down the hall and their hushed voices as they spoke to each other.

"Why did you tell her she would only wear the collar for a few days?" the male said in a low, hushed baritone.

Jin's chuckle was dry and lifeless. "Because she won't live for much longer than that. I don't care what Leo says. She won't conform. You can smell her male all over her. She's a mated female."

"None of the chosen were mated," the male argued.

"Apparently she's a fast-moving bitch."

"Faster than you?" The male chuckled and then made a low grunting sound as if he'd been hit.

"Fuck you, asshole. The only way I move fast is when I lay in for the kill."

"I'll remember that about you," he said. "And I'll steer clear of Leo when he gets a good whiff of the male on her."

"No shit. He's going to be fucking pissed as hell. Although more than likely by now, Chantelle is probably a widow."

The knife that once stabbed at Chan's brain now twisted painfully in her gut. If anyone laid a paw on Josh, she would personally see to their death. She ignored their sounds when they knocked on another door down the hall. The intense smell of outrage that suddenly seeped from her pores made Chan's eyes water. She walked into the bathroom and stared at the collar wrapped around her neck.

She lifted her hair and turned to see the small piece of metal now clasped around the buckle that secured the leather strap to her neck. When she touched it with her fingers, a zap of electricity burnt her fingertips.

"Bitch," she hissed, pulling her fingers away quickly and then sucking on them. She stared at her outraged expression in the mirror. "Chill out with the temper, Chan," she ordered herself. "Think clearly and figure out how the hell to get out of this nightmare."

Chapter Thirteen

ଽୠ

Josh would owe the owls big time once this was all over. He stalked warily down the street, keeping his gaze low. Focusing on the sound of his boots creating a steady rhythm on the sidewalk, he pulled the brim of his cowboy hat low. If any human were to see the intense glow in his eyes right now, or the snarl that was permanently fixed on his face ever since Chan disappeared, they would scream in fright.

A few more blocks and he reached the edge of town. It had been years since he'd been in such a warm climate. He didn't get why humans who lived in this region wore such cumbersome clothing. But they did. And he needed to fit in.

Someone stepped out of the alley and stopped in the middle of the sidewalk, facing him.

"Your cell phone isn't on." Thad scowled at him and then fell into stride alongside Josh. "Dover and Tyton flew over Fountain Hills. The place is swarming with leopards."

"There aren't any out this way." They crossed a narrow, two-lane highway and headed away from town. "And Chan isn't here."

"You sure?"

Josh ignored Thad's questioning look. If she were anywhere in this small human town, he would have smelled her. And he'd just finished walking every fucking street. "I'm sure."

"Did you contact her litter?"

Josh stared the length of the quiet highway that would lead to Phoenix. Not that he planned on walking the distance in these fucking cowboy boots. "Charles hasn't seen her. He's keeping his nose to the ground but isn't going to tell his mate. She's due to have a litter any day now."

"We can put a few leopards in the area, make sure her litter is protected." Thad pulled out his cell phone. "I'm still pissed I couldn't narrow the ISP down to a specific address. But at least this town isn't that big," he said as he pushed buttons on his cell phone. "Leo Pard posted that message on the PI site from somewhere in this town. We'll find him."

Josh nodded. He was impressed as hell how his species came together to help find the missing leopards. After the ambush at his cabin, the owls followed the leopards who took Chan, making it as far as the airport. Unfortunately, not even an owl could pace a plane. What they did learn though was Chan wasn't the only leopard ripped away from her litter, or in this case, from him.

Although the moment he found her...Chan would be his...permanently.

His blood burned. Every inch of him tingled with charged, angry energy that demanded to be released. Staying in his human form was harder to do than it ever had been in his life. His female was yanked out of his home and the fucking bastards who stole her from him would suffer long and hard before he finally killed them.

A semi-truck approached them on the highway. Josh felt the road vibrate through his boots and watched as the truck came closer and then finally passed him.

"I must be getting delirious from lack of sleep," Josh growled. "But I swear that was a leopard driving the human truck."

"I just thought the same thing." Thad looked over his shoulder. "I've never known a leopard to hold down a human job like that."

"They wouldn't. Unless they were seriously castrated." Josh glanced over his shoulder at the truck. No leopard would be able to tolerate sitting in the confinement of a truck cab for long hours. It would be like being fucking caged.

"Are you planning on walking by every rural house out here?" Thad held his hand over his eyes and squinted at the rugged land spreading out around them.

"If I have to."

"We got word that a lot of leopards flew into Phoenix. Race sniffed around the airport and swore he saw tons of dog crates being loaded onto a semi, except he smelled leopards and not canines." Thad glanced at Josh and then the two of them looked behind them.

"What the fuck," Josh hissed, stopping and turning as he frowned at the semi, which was a good ways down the highway, stopped and appeared to be turning around.

"You ever see a semi pull a U in the middle of a highway before?" Thad asked.

"Nope." And something told him not to stand around and see if this one jack-knifed or not. "What do you want to bet we're the reason he's trying to flip that damned thing? Let's not wait to find out."

"I'm with you. Let's get the hell out of here."

They bounded across the rough ground away from the highway. Something told Josh there was a reason the truck suddenly decided to turn around right after passing them. He looked in the direction the truck came from, squinting at the few ranch houses that sat off the highway.

The ground dipped and Josh stopped, standing in an old creek bed as he took his time sniffing the air.

"What is it?" Thad asked, glancing around them as well.

The truck finally successfully turned around and then pulled to the side of the road. No one got out, but Josh squatted in the gully and listened to his suddenly pounding heart. For once he ached to see something, be given some kind of sign, witness anything in his mind that would send him in the right direction.

"She's out here. Somewhere." He shook his head and then scratched his scalp. Tingles rushed over his body. He was charged, electrified with feral energy that craved an outlet. Urges more powerful that he'd ever experienced before crawled through him. "See if you can get a signal. Let's send the owls out and see what they glimpse over this way."

Thad nodded and pulled out his phone. He then glanced past Josh and nodded. "We've got company."

Josh turned as the driver of the semi walked around the front of the truck and then trotted across the highway and into the field toward them.

"Looks like another fucking leopard is going to bite the dust." He needed to release some of the energy that was on extreme overload inside him. "Come here, motherfucker. I can use the exercise."

Thad didn't comment but instead spoke quietly into his phone addressing Dover, telling him where they were and then asking if he wouldn't mind flying over and seeing if anything looked out of the ordinary.

Josh half listened while he watched the stout male head toward them. He waited until he could see the male's eyes, and then watched him sniff the air while shifting his gaze around the field. The male shot his attention to Josh when he stood and made himself visible.

"You lost?" he asked the asshole.

The male stopped walking and didn't say anything. Josh jumped out of the ravine and took a few steps toward the male who watched him warily. "I asked you a question, motherfucker."

Josh stiffened when the male moved his hand, rubbing it against the side of his dirty jeans. The breeze shifted and the smell of anger surprised Josh. He expected fear or possibly arrogance, but not anger. Josh stood an inch or so taller than the male, but otherwise he would guess them a pretty even match. Not that he worried for a moment he couldn't take the bastard out. His fury over losing Chan was so ripe it could probably be smelled all the way to Phoenix. Leopards were serious predators, killers by nature. They were aggressive and fought not only to defend what was theirs but also for pleasure.

Josh moved in on the male, willing to kill him in their skin and not take the time to change. Even though his blood boiled and his spine popped and burned, he wouldn't waste a moment that could be used searching for Chan. There wasn't time to create ceremony and fight according to protocol. These were leopards without honor, and he wouldn't treat them any other way.

"Why did you turn your truck around?" Josh asked, closing in on the male. "Tell me where my female is. There's no reason holding out on the truth at this point. In a few minutes nothing you've been ordered to do will matter to you."

The male still remained mute. Josh didn't have time to react when the male pulled a gun out of his back pocket, aimed it at Josh and fired.

* * * * *

Chan followed Jin and the male who had come to her room earlier down the stairs. She glanced behind her at the many closed doors that lined the upstairs hallway. Her senses were in full force again finally and she smelled leopards everywhere, males and females. Their confusion, pain, anger and hostility tore at her heart. This was bigger than simply finding Josh and running. Her kind were being abused in this place, and it wasn't acceptable. Somehow she needed to stop it. If she only had a clue what the fuck to do about all of this.

"He's in there." Jin pointed to a large, dark mahogany-wood door that remained closed. The same male who was with her before stood by her side, and she didn't meet Chan's gaze as she pointed, or look exceptionally happy. If anything, there was little smell of satisfaction on the female, as if possibly she weren't thrilled by her assigned chores.

"Thank you," Chan said quietly, pulling her gaze easily away from Jin and grabbed the large doorknob, pushing open the door.

Several male leopards turned as she entered. Chan felt a moment of hesitation but wouldn't let any of them smell weakness on her. She entered, leaving the door partially open and clasped her hands behind her back. There wasn't any point in saying anything, she wasn't the one requesting to be here.

"Leave us." Leo glared at the other males who all turned their attention to her.

"Is this the one?" one of them asked.

"I said leave," he growled harshly.

None of them flinched, but they didn't turn on him either. Chan stepped out of the way as they filed out of the room.

"Close the door behind you." Leo walked over to a counter and began typing on a laptop set up there. "We're going to make a few things clear."

Chan pressed her hand against the door, pushing it closed behind her while studying the male who now had his back to her. He wasn't unattractive, although there was something grossly compelling about his smell. It was as if his domination consumed him with so much intensity that there was barely room inside the shell of his body to contain it. While most leopards were naturally blonde, sometimes with highlights, his hair seemed almost white. His voice matched the male in her visions and she wondered why she didn't notice such a noticeable trait in him before.

When he turned around, pale turquoise eyes pinned her, his pupils no more than narrow slits. While most leopards worked hard to make their eyes appear human while in human form, apparently Leo didn't see the need.

He didn't smile. "How are you feeling?"

She didn't move when he approached but forced herself to remain relaxed with her hands clasped behind her back and the door behind her. "Okay," she lied.

Leo nodded once. "Good. You and I will become very close, and so we'll trust each other and never lie." He tilted his head slightly, his light-colored lashes barely covering his turquoise eyes as he focused on her collar. He brushed his finger over the band, pressing the leather against her neck. "Therefore I want you to know that we found the male who's been fucking you. He's been killed."

She checked her emotions quickly. "That's a shame. He was a good leopard."

"That's it? His scent is all over you. You've mated." He searched her face carefully.

The smell of his domination was intense. Chan stepped around him, moving slowly through the room and making a show of inspecting it. She was overly aware of him watching her backside and his gaze sent unpleasant tingles over her flesh.

"We're not mated." He didn't comment on her first lie and she fought desperately to keep her emotions under wrap and her heart beating slowly as she lazily waved her hand in the air. "I'm sure you know good sex sometimes leaves a mark on the male and female. It will pass."

"Very interesting." He moved behind her although his scent remained overwhelming no matter where he stood in the room. "Obviously all the research in the world can't allow you to know a female, or male, perfectly until you meet. I would have guessed you a bit more compassionate."

She turned around, although not quickly, and narrowed her gaze on him, giving all her attention to feeling hard and cold. "I'm very compassionate. I care very much for myself and my own well-being. Isn't that how all leopards are?"

For the first time he smiled and then surprisingly he actually laughed. "I smell the truth of your words," he said.

"And it makes sense you would feel that way. That is exactly how I feel."

She nodded, breathing out slowly, very slowly, and then taking her time inhaling. Taking too much of his scent into her lungs would make her puke.

"I'm going to answer your most obvious questions first, Chantelle." He waved his hand in the air, as if he expected her to say something, and gestured for her to be silent. Leo walked over to the large windows that covered the back wall of the high-ceilinged room and clasped his hands behind his back. "A little over thirty years ago, I saw the extinction of our species. It was the most unsettling vision. Every vision I had as a cub always came true. It wasn't until I reached maturity that I learned to master them and then use them to tame the future, make it bow down to me. Once I possessed this skill, I knew the only way for our species to survive was to create more like me."

She didn't say anything. But then what was there to say? *You're a bastard and I can't think of anything I'd rather do than sink my teeth into your neck until I puncture your jugular and you bleed to death?*

Chan stood there, forcing her hands to stay relaxed as she held them behind her back. More than anything she wanted to cross them over her chest, shield herself somehow. The plain white T-shirt made her feel exposed. No bra gave her the sensation of being half naked in his presence.

But the worst of it was fighting with every bit of her strength not to dwell on his words about Josh. If she let the pain lash through her, let her heart bleed over the loss of the only male who'd ever reached so deep inside her, then she would break down. And to do so would allow this leopard to crush her. Chan didn't have a clue what to expect in the next hour, or the next day, but she knew beyond a doubt that keeping her cool, bluffing as long as possible, would help her get through this despicable nightmare. She remained silent, waiting for him to continue and doing her best not to gag on the despicable smell of his insanity.

"It sucked that my mate was an idiot. She was fucking hot as hell, but not good for much more than giving me pleasure. She sure as hell wasn't going to give me any offspring. I wouldn't allow it." Leo turned around and she straightened, pinning her attention to his. He walked toward her slowly. "I spent several years searching for the smartest females, ones worthy of bearing my cubs. It took quite a bit of work, but I found them. They birthed my cubs. But allowing their mates to raise them, to pollute their brains with their idiotic beliefs would be wrong, don't you agree?"

Chan didn't have a clue what he was talking about. The glow of his pale eyes unnerved her though, and she hesitated before answering.

Apparently her silence didn't bother him. "You'll come to understand all of this in time. Although there are many of you with visions, just a few of you are truly special. And of course that is because you are mine. What I want you to know was that it was imperative the parents of my cubs not raise them. I would rather they grow up learning about the world on their own than having leopards who were no match to me pollute my cubs' minds with ridiculous beliefs and ideals. I know today I made the right decision. Look at you. You're perfect."

Chan studied his face, hearing his words and fighting to keep her mouth shut and not ask questions. She didn't want to hear the answers. There was no way she would believe he was trying to tell her he'd raped her mother then killed her parents so she would be forced to grow up an orphan. She continued with her slow breaths and focused on her heart beating. She wouldn't allow it to pound in her chest, or her outrage to grow as she struggled with the meanings to his words.

"Jin has explained the collar to you?" he asked, his expression relaxed as if he hadn't just unloaded some of the filthiest-smelling crap on her she'd ever heard or smelled.

"Yes," she said, keeping her tone flat.

"It's an age-old device actually, used by humans for centuries." He walked over to her again, dropping his gaze to her neck and then lower. "I confess it looks very attractive on you, somehow erotic. There's something about a collared female that does something to a male." Again he stroked the leather with his finger, gently pressing the collar against her flesh as he moved his finger back and forth around the curve of it. "I don't want to take it off of you. But I promise that I won't use it as a discipline device as long as you do everything I say. Sound good?"

"Sounds fine," she said quietly. She didn't look at his face, instead focused where she guessed his jugular pumped with his defiled blood. If he saw her eyes, she was sure he would see the anger that burned painfully through her soul.

Leo chuckled. "I see how you fight to restrain yourself."

Her heart skipped a beat. She didn't smell her emotions on her. If anything, all she smelled was Josh. As if that weren't painful enough.

"Which is fine," he continued, letting his finger slide off her collar and down her neck to her collarbone. "Trust comes with time. But you'll learn quickly that I'm the only male in your life who can keep you alive. We'll start with dinner. That will be a perfect opportunity for you to show everyone the bond that is already strong between the two of us. You'll sit next to me, and although you'll be served, you won't feed yourself. You won't eat a thing unless I feed it to you. Understand, Chantelle?"

"I understand."

"Good." He let his finger fall down her front, pressing into her shirt as he dragged it over her heart, which thumped with the outrage she fought to restrain.

She feared it would take more than a collar to keep her from attacking the pompous bastard who was getting a bit too friendly with his touch. He pressed his finger against her chest bone, as if pointing to the very source deep inside her that ached to attack and destroy.

"Once you pass your first lessons in trust, we'll see about a new wardrobe," he said gently, his soft tone oozing with false compassion that made her blood curdle. "Maybe I'll have Jin take you shopping for something sexy here in the next few days. She's jealous of you, you know. Jin wants to be by my side, but she doesn't understand her duties are as equally important as yours are."

"I won't do anything to upset her." Chan matched his soft tone. She wondered if Jin warning her to run wasn't out of compassion, but possibly for more selfish reasons that Chan wasn't aware of.

Leo let his hand fall to his side, not saying anything, although she smelled his warped sense of amusement. Possibly he was one of those males who got his rocks off thinking that females would fight to be by his side and be jealous of each other while feigning friendship simply to please him. Her stomach turned as she imagined what kind of male Leo was. Although all of this personal information about him was probably good to know, none of it helped her figure out a way to get out of here. She glanced toward the tall windows, noting there wasn't any way to open them. She would have to change, leap through them and run as fast as she could. Although being zapped with electricity might make that plan a bit faulty.

"Shall we go eat?" Leo stood at the door and extended his hand to her.

Chan didn't smile but kept her expression neutral as she followed him out of the office.

* * * * *

It was a damned good thing she'd been ordered not to feed herself. Chan never knew such intense humiliation as she sat next to Leo, who lounged at the head of the long dining room table. She sat to his right and Jin to his left. Four males sat at the other seats and a small group of leopards hurried in and out of the room, serving and refilling glasses, bringing food on dishes that probably cost a small fortune. There was no way Chan would be able to swallow a single bite of any of the food served. She hated how the males gawked at her, Jin gave her guarded looks and Leo sat proudly at the head of the table, glancing at her occasionally as if she were his prized possession.

"How many on the list have survived to this point?" Leo sliced a sharp knife through a thick piece of steak before putting a large portion of it into his mouth.

"We've got thirteen." The male sitting next to Jin looked familiar. "Seven of them were killed."

"Damn shame. None of the good ones, I hope."

"Only one from the top ten didn't make it," Jin said, eyeing Chan, and Chan's untouched plate curiously before stabbing her own steak with her knife, bringing the whole thing to her mouth. She ripped part of it off with extended teeth and then sucked it into her mouth.

"That's a shame." Leo frowned although there was a level of sarcasm in his tone that was nauseating.

"Tore pulled in the last three," one of the males at the end of the table said. "They gave him a bit of a challenge, but I got there in time to help contain them."

"They gave you problems?" Leo raised his eyebrow at the male next to Jin, who was Tore. Chan remembered now he was one of the males at Birdie's house.

"They teamed up with each other and attacked me. I was able to restrain all of them, but not without killing one of them." He didn't show any remorse, or seem concerned this bit of information might offend Leo.

"The number thirteen bothers me," Jin said, running her tongue over her lips and then glancing again at Chan's plate before meeting Chan's indifferent gaze. "We only want the strong ones. If any of them show any signs of weakness, they die."

If that was meant as a threat to Chan, she didn't allow her emotions or expression to register any sign of concern.

"We'll start the testing tomorrow. You'll have your chance to sort the stronger from the weaker ones." Leo patted Jin's hand.

Chan wasn't sure, but it seemed Jin's smile toward Leo wasn't sincere. Maybe she imagined it. Leo didn't seem perturbed by the female's expression. Instead, he turned to Chan, acknowledging her for the first time since they all started eating. Lifting the fork from next to her plate, he used his own knife to slice through her steak. Then raising a small piece of the meat to her lips, he offered it to her.

Chan sucked the recently killed beef into her mouth, keeping her gaze locked with his but harboring her emotions. As rich and juicy as the tender piece of cow flesh was, her insides churned. It was going to be hard as hell keeping her repulsion toward him hidden if he kept her by his side much longer. She would much rather have bitten off his finger than accept the piece of meat from his hand.

"Are we going to test them all at the same time?" Tore asked. He watched Chan with a mixture of curiosity and arousal as Leo continued feeding her. "Sounds like we're lucky we don't have to participate in those tests and can move straight to the breeding stage."

"They will all test together at first. You'll join them once we know who are compatible to be with you." Leo put Chan's fork down on her plate and picked up her roll. Tearing it with his fingers, he then pressed a small morsel of it to her lips. He smelled pleased as hell when she accepted the food from his fingers, and watched her while answering Tore's question. "While they sleep, we'll hook them up to our equipment so we can register and record how they react during visions. We've tested everything so there shouldn't be any problem distinguishing between dreams and visions. Once we've established who has the most visions, the second stage of recording the visions and then interpreting them will begin."

"What if they don't have visions?" the male at the end of table asked.

"We've been through this, Ben," Jin said, her exasperation smelling stale. "We don't need leopards who don't have visions. Those who make it through all four stages will then enter into the procreation stage."

Chan looked at her but then blinked and fought to swallow her roll, which was like dry paste in her mouth. Jin was obviously quicker at catching Chan's emotions than Leo had been.

"That's right, my dear," she purred, looking at Chan. "You are going to be the mother to a new race of leopards, a species bred with the power to make us stronger than any other breed out there. You'll go down in history as a female who littered a new hybrid."

Chan tried to swallow but almost choked. Leo lifted her glass of milk to her lips, holding it carefully while she struggled to drink without dribbling it down her chin. More than anything she wanted to grab the glass, down what she could and then hurl the glass into his face. Or maybe at Jin. Hearing the glass shatter in her mind and seeing the sharp, tiny pieces rip at their flesh while she indulged in her violent daydream did little to settle her nerves.

"You'll be right there with her, Jin. You know you will." Again when Leo patted her hand, Jin seemed rather put out. In fact this time, she moved her hand from underneath his and reached for her knife. She stabbed her meat as Leo's cell phone rang. He seemed less than interested that his false praise wasn't appreciated by Jin, and pulled his phone from his waist. "Yes, what is it?" he said calmly, but his scent changed as quickly as his expression did. "That isn't possible," he hissed. "We've already confirmed their deaths."

His pale turquoise eyes flickered with sparks of pale green when he slowly lifted his face. Chan watched him, as did everyone else at the table. The leopards moving around the table, refilling serving dishes and clearing away plates even stopped moving as the overwhelming smell of anger made her eyes water.

"Stop them now, no matter what it takes," he growled, his face blotching with rosettes as his fury escalated. His eyes grew wide and his mouth opened as he stared at the end of the table.

Chan turned her head just in time to see a parliament of owls flying toward the long windows at the end of the room. Instinctively she ducked when they flew right through the glass.

Chapter Fourteen

ဆ

Outrage flooded Josh's system when he leapt at the front door. Wood splintered and crashed, the sound echoing in a luxurious-looking foyer. Or at least it was until he crashed into it in his fur.

Race and Thad were right behind him, but he didn't pay any attention as he walked over the broken wood scattered over the smooth, cool floor and sniffed out the place. His claws clicked against the marble underneath him until he reached a carpeted hallway. The smell of leopards was so thick in the house he wasn't sure which door to slam through next.

He was saved the trouble when one of them opened and a male stepped out in his flesh. Race leapt, roaring loudly as he went straight for the neck. The male screamed, covering his face and doing his best to change and retreat at the same time. There were others behind him and Josh plowed through each one of them, grabbing arms, legs, torsos, whatever he could reach first, digging in with his teeth and then hurling them fiercely across the room.

Only one of them managed to change into his fur. Two lay not moving and he really didn't give a rat's ass where the others disappeared to. He attacked on auto drive, willing and more than capable of killing every fucking leopard in the house if he had to until he found Chan. His outrage and adrenaline pumped through his veins hard enough he didn't even feel the pain from the bullet wound in his shoulder.

The male in his fur only got to leap once. *Bring it on, motherfucker*, Josh growled, and attacked without mercy. He threw the male against the wall hard enough to knock several framed paintings to the ground. They crashed and somewhere in the back of his brain it registered that a female screamed. The male didn't move and then slowly changed back to his human form, dead.

Josh almost retreated from the room, ready to plow through the other doors searching for Chan, when he froze. She stood next to a table, which was covered with fine dining ware and crystal. The chair behind her was knocked over and her hands covered her mouth. He stalked toward her, ready to take what was his and get the hell out of there. Nothing else mattered.

"Don't move any closer, Josh, or she suffers dearly." There was another female in the room.

Josh turned on her, snarling, and glared at her overly made-up face and dyed black hair. It was Jin Rose, and her nervousness smelled so salty it turned his stomach. She gripped a small black box on her belt and shifted her attention from him to Chan.

"Tell him to back off, Chantelle. Do it now," the female warned.

"Josh. The collar on my neck—the box on her belt controls it. Don't hurt her, please." Chan's voice quavered.

"That's right, kitty cat. One wrong move and I fry your piece of tail."

Chan's pleading tone contradicted her spicy-hot outrage. But the painted slut's venomous words didn't match her worried, almost paranoid smell. And this time she wasn't covering her scent with human perfumes and leather. Josh curled his lip at the painted hussy, ignoring her when her fingers hovered over the box at her hip.

Something crashed above them. Howls and screams echoed through the house. Glass shattered and wood cracked as the house sounded as if it were being completely destroyed. Not that any of it mattered to Josh.

He moved in slowly on the female who glared at him, her gaze flicking from him to Chan. She stepped sideways, continually fingering the box at her hip.

"Tell him to back off," she shrieked as her nervousness pierced the air around her.

"He's not going to listen. God, Jin. Just let us go, please," Chan begged.

Jin's laugh pissed him off as much as Chan's pleading did. No one he cared for would ever need to beseech another for mercy. He lunged at Jin.

She screamed and jumped on to the table, starting to change as dishes and glasses shattered and their contents spilled all over the place. Chan grabbed her neck, howling in pain when Josh jumped on to the table too, breaking it in two under his incredible weight.

Jin's clothes ripped, exposing her breasts and a tattoo on her right arm before black rosettes covered her body and then fur flowed over her sensual curves. Her belt buckle popped loose and the belt slid off her body—with the box on it. She tried reaching for it with her mouth, but it slid through the broken table and fell to the floor along with broken glass and spilled food.

Josh ignored the broken table. He leapt off it and over to where Chan crouched on the ground, still in her human form. Her fingers were wrapped around the collar fixed to her neck so tight he could barely see it. Josh ran his tongue over her hair, tasting her sadness, her pain, and beneath it, the beautiful, sexy lady he so quickly had fallen hard for. He licked her again when he breathed in his scent, which clung heavily to her in spite of her other emotions.

Chan let go of her collar, her expression tight with pain and discomfort, and pushed her hair from her face to look at him. She reached for him, ready to stroke his massive head, when a crashing sound made her jump and scream.

Josh flipped around, guarding her from anyone who might try to attack. She needed to change. He smelled her pain, her fear, and wondered if possibly the trauma of whatever she'd endured while she was here affected her too strongly for her to transform out of her human state.

Jin jumped in between the broken table, causing more plates to crash, and struggled to get under part of the table still standing.

"Don't let her get the belt. Josh, please!" The urgency in Chan's tone was enough to make Josh dive at the female.

The belt was curled under the broken table like a coiled snake. Jin grabbed it with her teeth and he lunged at her, sending part of the table flying sideways. Jin howled when one of the legs tried impaling her in the gut. When she jumped out of its way, she fell over sideways against another leg. The long table, with all of its trimming, had turned into a discombobulated maze requiring some extensive acrobats to get around.

Josh didn't have time for bullshit. He bulldozed through the table, breaking off one of the legs, and smashed into Jin. She dropped the belt out of her mouth and attacked full force with all claws and teeth. But she was half his size and it took little effort to lift her with his mouth and throw her across the room.

Grabbing the belt in his mouth, he leapt over the table again and searched for Chan.

"Let's get out of here," she yelled, hurrying over to him. To his surprise, she grabbed his coat, digging her fingers into his shoulders, and straddled him. "I can't change," she cried, burying her face in his coat. "I thought the drug was out of my system," she added, and then the salty smell of her tears filled the air.

It was all Josh could do not to rise up on his hind legs and roar with outrage. He wanted to level the whole goddamned house. Not only did they steal his female, they hurt her too.

Anger ripped at him so hard that for a moment he feared he would take off too aggressively and knock her off him.

Hold on tight, my love, he growled, and worked his way around the destroyed room.

The large windows were shattered and glass cracked underneath his weight, cutting his paws. He ignored the pain. Chan wrapped her arms around his neck so fiercely, holding on with all of her strength, and pushed against the gun shot wound that he'd yet to take time to tend to. Again, he simply used the pain that shot through him to feed his adrenaline. It added to his determination to get them out of there. Once they were safe, once he knew Chan was okay, then he would worry about his own wounds.

Rough angles of glass were stuck to the panes and tore his skin when he jumped through it. Chan squealed and held on tighter, gripping his waist with her thighs. He fought the urge to roar, or turn his head and make sure she was okay. But he wouldn't lose the belt in his mouth. Whatever that fucking thing was around her neck, the box on the belt controlled it. The sooner he got that damned collar off her neck, the better.

They leapt through the yard just as more crashing sounded inside. There was a mixture of roars and yelling, and he needed to make sure Thad and Race were okay. As well as the owls. But first, Chan needed to be taken away from the monster who'd put a collar on her. The bastard would die for that.

With nothing but open, undeveloped land surrounding the large mansion basically out in the middle of nowhere, it made it hard to run anywhere where he wouldn't be easily spotted.

"Josh, they're chasing us. You've got to run faster," Chan screamed at him.

If he ran any faster she would fall off. He growled, protesting, and taking no more than a second to turn and glance over his shoulder for fear she would slide off him.

"Give me the belt." Already her body slid on his back and she squealed, digging her knees into his sides, but stubbornly tried taking the belt from his mouth.

The bull-headed little female would end up falling off him and be skinned alive on the rough ground in her flesh.

"Give it to me," she hissed when he wouldn't release it from his mouth. "I'm going to fasten it around your neck. No one can get it from you then."

Good idea. Bad timing. He didn't want her doing anything but holding on with everything she had. She pulled so hard on the belt though, if he didn't let her have it, it would fall and they would have to stop to retrieve it. Some day soon they were going to have a real long talk about how she needed to quit trying to control everything. It made it really hard to protect her.

There were leopards chasing them, but apparently Thad and Race were part of the crowd. They were closing in on the mountains and dangerously close to human towns and scattered rural houses when Chan finally secured the belt to his neck. She wrapped her arms securely around his neck. He loved how her body molded with his, but knew she held on to keep warm and to keep from falling off more than she did to snuggle.

At the first large boulders, he slowed, not wanting to risk racing up the mountain and hurting her more than she already was. She slid off him just as the ground pounded under his feet from leopards approaching from behind.

"Josh! Watch out," she screamed.

He turned on her, snarling. *Get behind the fucking rocks and don't move!*

For once she seemed to listen to him as she stared at him with glowing green eyes and slowly placed her hands on a large rock. Her gaze shifted quickly though and a scream barely ripped from her throat when Josh caught sight of a male leaping toward him through his peripheral vision.

The male was in midair when Thad body-slammed him from the side, sending the two of them rolling over the ground. Owls flew around them, dive-bombing several of the leopards who'd managed to follow them this far. And Race was there too, eager to fight and take down as many as he could.

The male behind the one Race tackled was older than Josh and although thicker, was also not as tall. His teeth were sharp as hell and tore at Josh's hide when Josh tried to send him flying. Another leopard came at him, but then a loud explosion made Chan scream behind him.

Josh's adrenaline spiked with such a rush his entire body seemed charged with electricity. He felt it tingle through his veins, hitting every nerve ending and spearing deep into his gut. He went up on his hind legs and swatted hard with his front paw, sending the older leopard tumbling to the side and into one of the other leopards. That's when he saw Leo, standing back a good twenty yards and with a large gun.

Human weapons weren't one of his specialties. He'd never known a leopard who spent too much time with them. It seemed odd to him that Leo, this male who claimed to want to organize the best of the best of his species, would have one and be ready to use it. But then he'd found it equally as weird earlier when the semi-driving male pulled a gun and shot him. It was a damn good thing he wasn't that good at using one and just grazed Josh's shoulder. Nonetheless, it hurt like hell and he didn't plan on getting hit again with one of those bullets.

"Josh! Get over here now! He's going to kill you!" The urgency in Chan's voice made his hair stand on end. "God, please. I can't lose you. Please."

All of the screaming, howling, guns firing and bodies slamming suddenly faded into another world. Chan's overwhelming scent, the unique smell they'd created together the last time they made love, filled his lungs. It was the smell of her love. Whether she voiced it or not, Josh knew without any doubts his female loved him as much as he loved her.

212

He turned, leaping forward and managing to dodge the leopard who tried jumping on him. As he landed behind the rock next to Chan, the male who tried attacking him hissed in pain when a bullet, more than likely meant for Josh, grazed the male's side.

Chan looked up at him, her eyes glowing as black rosettes slowly covered her body.

Get out of your clothes, my little cat, he growled, using his body and the rock as a shield for her.

Chan pulled her jeans off as quickly as she could and barely managed to yank the shirt from her head before her body changed, contorting and covering with different shades of fur before she fell to all fours.

Josh scooped her clothes into his mouth. *Let's get the fuck out of here.*

* * * * *

The sun glared at him on the horizon when Josh looked away from the fence and watched Chan walk toward him.

"It looks like there's going to be ten for supper," she told him, smiling and then surveying the tall privacy fence that now lined the immediate property surrounding his cabin. "I hate the coil going along the top. It makes it look like some kind of confine."

"I agree." He pulled her into his arms, inhaling her sweet scent and then kissed the top of her head. "The barbed wire will have to do for now. I'm still working on setting up the monitoring system."

"I know security is important, but what about building on to the cabin?" She tilted her head back to look up at him and her long hair tumbled over his arms. "We're going to need more room."

"Are you sure this is the life you want?" He petted her hair and grew hard as he breathed in her scent—like honey, mixed with the smell of the meat she'd been preparing for supper.

Chan laughed. "You've asked me that a hundred times. We're a solitary species, but if we're going to fight Leo and help others to learn about him and steer clear of his traps, then what we're doing here is important."

"Not every female would share her home with other leopards. There will be other females here as well as males."

"I know that." She made a face at him, puckering her lips together and draining all blood in his body straight to his cock. "We can build on to our cabin. But it might be a good idea to also build a few small cabins on the land too. There will be litters showing up at times. They will want their privacy."

Ever since they returned to Minnesota, to his cabin by Lake of the Woods, phone calls came tumbling in. Race and Thad kept in close touch, but there were others, leopards who were on the list created by Leo and who'd escaped the day he pulled Chan out of there. They broke and destroyed her collar, and other males and females reported in doing the same. But Leo was still out there, and although quiet at the moment, Josh didn't doubt for a moment he would surface again.

"It will take time and money, but we'll make this little cabin into a home you'll be proud of."

"I'm already proud of it," she whispered, and went up on tiptoe, leaning against him to kiss him. "Are you satisfied with the blood tests?"

After telling him what Leo mentioned, his implication that he raped females to create cubs he viewed would be worthy of calling his own, Chan wouldn't be comfortable until she knew they weren't related. They owed it to their parents to prove Leo told nothing more than terrible lies.

"Very satisfied," he growled, nipping at her lip. "I don't know if we'll ever know what Leo meant by that grumbling bullshit he fed you."

"Whatever it was, he believed it." Chan's expression sobered and she looked up at him with sensual pools of green that sparkled like emeralds from the sun. "He won't bother us again. Not with this security system you've installed around us."

"So much better to keep you trapped in my den, little cat," he snarled, and scooped her into his arms, loving the sound of her laughter and vowing he would do what it took to hear that sound daily for the rest of his life. "How long until everyone shows up?"

"Not long," she said, still laughing when he used his foot to kick open their cabin door. "Less than an hour maybe."

"Then we don't have much time." The past couple weeks were like this. He didn't want to live his life rushing, but with getting her apartment in Seattle emptied, bringing her things here and trying to secure the cabin and ensure their safety, he'd barely had time to sit and relax.

But there were some things he would make time for. Chan slid down his body while he pushed the door shut with his foot. Then grabbing her loose sweater, he yanked at it, tugging until he pulled it over her head. She wasn't wearing a bra and her full, round breasts bounced before him while her nipples hardened instantly.

The pressure lengthening in his cock made it damned hard to move, let alone get his own clothes off. He needed inside Chan now.

"Get out of your clothes, my little cat, before I rip them off you," he growled, backing away from her to strip out of his clothes.

Chan didn't hesitate to obey. "You keep ripping my clothes off me and you'll have a hell of a fight on your hands when other males show up and I've been rendered naked," she teased, giggling while she sauntered away from him, shaking her hips and unzipping her jeans.

"Then we'll be a population of two," he grumbled.

"Oh really?" Her laugh was beautiful, peaceful and musical, and her happiness filled the room with such a clean smell.

He didn't mind a bit clouding it up with the sultry scent of their lust and love though. Chan managed to get out of her shoes and slid her jeans down her legs, giving him one hell of a view of her perfectly shaped ass when he grabbed her.

"Josh, I'm…Oh!" she cried out when he lifted her off the ground and pushed her against the wall with her jeans tangled around her legs. "I can't get them off," she laughed, twisting against him and rubbing her bare ass brutally against his cock.

"You've run out of time," he growled, pinning her with his body and burying his face in her hair while his cock seemed to find its own way between the soft cheeks of her ass.

"I hope I never run out of time," she purred, arching her back and twitching her ass like a cat would swat its tail.

He growled as her soft flesh tortured his cock. "Not with me, little cat. You can have all the time you want."

"Good." She turned her head, trying to see him over her shoulder and at the same time shift her body so she could turn around. "Give me what I want now and later I'm going to demand more of your time."

She was bossy. There wasn't any denying that. He could handle her though, and with time she would learn that what he said was meant out of his love for her. And she would listen. Right now was the perfect time to start.

He pressed her shoulder back against the wall and molded his hips against hers, pushing his cock deeper between her legs until he felt how soaked she was.

"Let me at least get out of my jeans," she complained, struggling against him.

The more she moved, the harder he became.

"You're fine just how you are." He loved the slope of her back, how warm her body was when he pressed against her.

"But I can't move."

"If you move much more, this will be over before it begins," he growled, and nipped at her shoulder.

Chan stilled although her breathing grew raspy, as if she purred and growled at the same time. "Not strong enough to handle it?" she growled, and then managed to slowly sway her hips against the wall.

"Damn it, female," he hissed, grabbing her hips and hoisting her higher against the wall.

Her jeans tangled around her ankles and she tried kicking to get them off. Something about confining her, getting her to accept submitting to him, even if it was just for a few minutes, made the struggle all the more worth it.

"My jeans," she wailed.

But he locked her legs between his and pinned her so his dick easily slid inside her.

"Oh God," she cried, turning her head so her cheek was flat against the wall and then turned the other way.

Her hair draped over her shoulders, wild and curly like a mane of long, blonde waves. Josh buried his face in it, breathing in the smell he'd grown to love more than any other scent he'd ever smelled before. And her pussy, so wet and tight, wrapped around his dick, sheathing it with a warm welcome that created a fire throughout his entire body.

"Don't move," he ordered, keeping his face buried over her shoulder with her hair tickling his face. He loved it though. Loved everything about her.

Even the defiant sigh she let out when she made an effort to relax. "How can I? You've got me pinned against the wall."

"Damned good place for you," he muttered, and began moving slowly inside her.

Her soaked muscles constricted against his shaft, soaking him further so her cream dripped over his balls and made them tighten with need. She might have relaxed her body, but with everything she had, he knew his little female did her best to tighten her pussy and keep him buried deep inside her.

"I can think of a few good places for you too," she growled.

"I might let you show me later."

"Let?" She chuckled as if the thought of obeying him amused her.

He thrust hard, feeling her ripple and then stretch to allow all of him inside. Chan howled and he growled his satisfaction. She would always need to feel that sense of control or power. It was her nature just as it was his to protect her, care and love her for the rest of his life.

"If you behave." He scraped her bare neck with his teeth and then sucked at the spot where her heartbeat pounded.

"Oh God," she whimpered, relaxing further as she convulsed around his cock. "Josh," she cried out, and then her orgasm hit.

He impaled her again, loving how her come washed over him in waves that were so warm, so creamy and thick. Chan dug her nails into the wall while her scent increased so that it filled the room with its wonderfully appealing, pungent scent.

With stroke after stroke the pressure built inside him, tightening his balls, creeping up his spine until he couldn't handle it any longer.

"Chan," he growled, biting her neck and then licking the spot where he'd bitten.

She moaned, doing her best to move against the wall, or crawl up it. Her pussy clung to his cock, soaking and milking him.

"I love you," he groaned, meaning every word as he spilled all he had inside her.

And just in time too. In spite of the thickness of their lovemaking in the air around them, the smell of other leopards reached his nose.

"Oh crap," Chan complained when he let her slide down the wall. She almost fell over her jeans when she grabbed her clothes and darted out of the living room.

Josh dressed, unable to pull the grin from his face, and then opened the door for his cousin. Like he cared if anyone knew he'd just enjoyed the best female his species had to offer.

Chan appeared, looking beautiful and ready to play hostess, just a short bit later. He turned when she walked into the kitchen, smiling at her freshly applied makeup and brushed hair. She walked right up to him and wrapped her arms around him.

"I love you," she whispered, but then got a very odd look on her face.

"That wasn't the look I imagined on your face when you finally told me that," he complained.

"I'm sorry. It's just that right after we met, I had this vision of leaning into you and telling you that I loved you."

His heart swelled with so much pride he could only look at her for a moment, adoring how beautiful she was as she glowed with embarrassment and, God yes, with love.

"When was this vision?" he asked, ignoring Thad and Race, who leaned against the counter making a blatant show of watching them.

She shook her head slowly, looking down toward his chest. "After we met," she offered.

"When?"

The next best thing to watching her face flush when she came was watching her expression turn defiant and determined when she looked up at him and glared.

"Right after we met. Right after I kicked your ass. Satisfied?"

Race snickered and then quickly looked down at his beer when Josh glared at him.

"Very satisfied." He pulled her into his arms and stroked her hair. "I've got the best damned female there is. Who could ask for more?"

Also by Lorie O'Clare

ଛ

About the Author

~

All my life, I've wondered at how people fall into the routines of life. The paths we travel seemed to be well-trodden by society. We go to school, fall in love, find a line of work (and hope and pray it is one we like), have children and do our best to mold them into good people who will travel the same path. This is the path so commonly referred to as the "real world".

The characters in my books are destined to stray down a different path other than the one society suggests. Each story leads the reader into a world altered slightly from the one they know. For me, this is what good fiction is about, an opportunity to escape from the daily grind and wander down someone else's path.

Lorie O'Clare lives in Kansas with her three sons.

Lorie welcomes comments from readers. You can find her website and email address on her author bio page at www.ellorascave.com.

Tell Us What You Think

We appreciate hearing reader opinions about our books. You can email us at Comments@EllorasCave.com.

Why an electronic book?

We live in the Information Age — an exciting time in the history of human civilization, in which technology rules supreme and continues to progress in leaps and bounds every minute of every day. For a multitude of reasons, more and more avid literary fans are opting to purchase e-books instead of paper books. The question from those not yet initiated into the world of electronic reading is simply: *Why?*

1. *Price.* An electronic title at Ellora's Cave Publishing and Cerridwen Press runs anywhere from 40% to 75% less than the cover price of the exact same title in paperback format. Why? Basic mathematics and cost. It is less expensive to publish an e-book (no paper and printing, no warehousing and shipping) than it is to publish a paperback, so the savings are passed along to the consumer.

2. *Space.* Running out of room in your house for your books? That is one worry you will never have with electronic books. For a low one-time cost, you can purchase a handheld device specifically designed for e-reading. Many e-readers have large, convenient screens for viewing. Better yet, hundreds of titles can be stored within your new library — on a single microchip. There are a variety of e-readers from different manufacturers. You can also read e-books on your PC or laptop computer. (Please note that Ellora's Cave does not endorse any specific brands.

You can check our websites at www.ellorascave.com or www.cerridwenpress.com for information we make available to new consumers.)

3. *Mobility.* Because your new e-library consists of only a microchip within a small, easily transportable e-reader, your entire cache of books can be taken with you wherever you go.

4. *Personal Viewing Preferences.* Are the words you are currently reading too small? Too large? Too... ANNOYING? Paperback books cannot be modified according to personal preferences, but e-books can.

5. *Instant Gratification.* Is it the middle of the night and all the bookstores near you are closed? Are you tired of waiting days, sometimes weeks, for bookstores to ship the novels you bought? Ellora's Cave Publishing sells instantaneous downloads twenty-four hours a day, seven days a week, every day of the year. Our webstore is never closed. Our e-book delivery system is 100% automated, meaning your order is filled as soon as you pay for it.

Those are a few of the top reasons why electronic books are replacing paperbacks for many avid readers.

As always, Ellora's Cave and Cerridwen Press welcome your questions and comments. We invite you to email us at Comments@ellorascave.com or write to us directly at Ellora's Cave Publishing Inc., 1056 Home Avenue, Akron, OH 44310-3502.

COMING TO A BOOKSTORE NEAR YOU!

ELLORA'S CAVE

Bestselling Authors Tour

CPSIA information can be obtained at www.ICGtesting.com
Printed in the USA
LVOW061053041011

249026LV00001B/91/P